Daddy Dom 3

Daddy Doctor To The Rescue

+

Connor's Little One

A DDLG and ABDL 2 in 1 novel collection

of kinky BDSM age play stories

By Tina Moore

Table of Contents

Daddy Doctor To The Rescue

A DDLG and ABDL romantic love story about a baby girl who becomes her Daddy Dom's favorite patient

By Tina Moore

Chapter 1

"Ms. Banks, you stand accused of possession of MDMA and public indecency. How do you plead?" The judge peered at me over the rim of his small, rectangular glasses. The look on his ancient face made it seem like he could see into my very soul, and he did not like what he saw there. What he saw was a scrawny, five-foot-nothing girl with unkempt black hair, a dirty black tank top, ripped black stockings and smeared mascara. It had been a rough night.

"Guilty, your Honor," I said, my voice cracking a bit. On the outside, I may have looked like a wild party girl, but the reality was that I was closer to a scared schoolgirl who had been sent to the principal's office. I didn't have much of a case, there was a video of the whole thing from the cop's body camera, and my lawyer thought I could get a better deal if I threw myself on the mercy of the court. The judge nodded, took off his glasses, and crossed his wrinkled hands, considering for a moment.

"Your court-appointed attorney filled me in on your history. Very sad to lose both of your parents so young. You grew up in foster care, and you've been in and out of jail ever since your foster parents threw you out last year. I don't see a permanent address listed here for you. Where are you staying currently?" Again, that soul-piercing gaze. I cleared my throat before speaking, hoping my voice wouldn't crack.

"With friends, your honor," I squeak.

"I see. Is there anything else you'd like to add or does that bring us more or less up to speed?" He questioned.

"It does your Honor," I reply. I know that I probably haven't made a very good impression, but I have no defense for my stupid actions. My "rap sheet" sounded more impressive than it actually was. Most of it was just dumb stunts done in an attempt to impress whatever boy had caught my eye that week. They never stuck around, though, no matter how impressive my stunts were.

"Well, I have some good news for you, although you may not see it as such at first. There is a rehab facility that specializes in troubled young women, such as yourself. Their technique is highly experimental, but it has yielded promising results. Rather than another fruitless stint in jail, I sentence you to thirty days of treatment at the Franken Institute for Young Women," he said.

Rehab?! I was astounded. I wasn't a junkie. I just liked to have a good time, get a little loose, and forget my troubles for a bit. I did not need rehab.

"But, sir -" I was cut off the judge's hammer signaling an end to the session. Everyone began to shuffle around, and my court-appointed attorney took off without so much as wishing me "good luck." There would be no appeal. The bailiff began escorting me back to holding. I sneered at him to cover up the fact that I just wanted to curl up into a ball and cry, hoping that I looked a lot tougher than I felt.

"A van will be along shortly to take you to

the facility," the bailiff said before shoving me roughly back into my cell. I sat on my hard cot and waited, trying to keep up a tough facade in case any of the other inmates were in the mood to start something. Inside, however, my mind was spinning. I had not meant to get arrested. No one ever does, I suppose. I had only agreed to hold on to ecstasy to impress Tyler, yet another in a long string of boys who I would never hear from again. I never even got to take any before getting busted. As soon as the handcuffs came out, Tyler and his friends were nowhere to be seen, and I was left to fend for myself. Typical, stupid me.

I lied down on the miserably hard cot. The long night of drinking and dancing was beginning to catch up to me, and I longed for sleep, yet I couldn't get comfortable on the hard cot. Even if I could, the disastrous night would keep repeating in my head anyway. The way Tyler and his friends kept egging me on, daring me to do more and more ridiculous things until I found myself flashing a cop while Tyler laughed and recorded me with his phone. That laughter was still ringing in my ears, mocking me. I covered my eyes and rolled over onto my side, trying to find a more comfortable position but a loose spring poked me in the rib. Hopefully, this rehab place would have decent beds. That would be something to look forward to, at least.

Chapter 2

I finally got some rest during the drive to the rehab facility, the gentle swaying of the van rocking me to sleep. I woke with a start as a pair of massive, rusty gates protested loudly as they slowly swung open. I looked out of the van windows to see a few sad trees peppered around a mostly empty parking lot.

What a dump. I rolled my eyes and slumped down in my seat, sulking. I knew that I should be grateful that I wasn't in jail, but I couldn't bring myself to be happy about being involuntarily confined with a bunch of drug addicts. Who knows what kind of dangerous freaks waited for me inside?

As we pulled up to the nondescript brick building, two orderlies opened the van door and looked at me expectantly. I knew what they wanted of me, but I was feeling particularly bratty, so I just sat there, not moving.

"Ms. Banks, step out of the vehicle, please," one of them said in the deep, commanding voice of someone who is used to being listened to. I stuck my tongue out at him before turning my face to the window and crossing my arms over my chest. I may have been court-ordered to be here, but I didn't have to make it easy for them.

Strong hands wrapped around my arms and before I knew it, I was over his shoulder! I could feel my skirt blow up, and I knew that my panties were being exposed for everyone to see. I knew he was trying to humiliate me, but this was hardly the first time I'd been ass-up in front of a crowd of people. My instinct was to give this guy an earful to let him know who he was dealing, but I stopped myself. I knew from experience that you could push these guys, but only so far before they "accidentally" sucker-punched you in the eye. I decided on a softer approach.

"They should put a saddle on you," I said as casually as possible.

"Your human rickshaw service only gets

two stars from me. I'm sorry to say. Bony shoulders, would not ride again," I angrily said.

"Shut up," he muttered and brought me inside. I grinned, feeling like I had gotten away with something. It may have been a stupid, small victory, but it was mine, and I was going to enjoy it. He came to a stop by the front desk and unceremoniously dumped me onto the floor. I landed badly on my ankle but didn't give him the satisfaction of letting on. Once upright, I saw that the place was a bit nicer on the inside. It had a cozy, if somewhat institutional, feel. There were oversized chairs and couches in the lobby and hotel art lining the walls. The carpet was a terrible lime green that looked so old. It probably should have been in a museum. I didn't mind it, however. It gave the place a bit more character.

Maybe this place won't be so bad after all. I dared to hope as I looked around.

A middle-aged woman in a sweater and khakis, who seemed to have been waiting for our arrival, saw us come in and approached us. She had a broad, matronly face and a name tag that said, "Deborah."

"Has this one been giving you trouble, Sam?" she said, assessing me with a cold, dispassionate gaze.

"Not too much, ma'am," he said. "Just some first day jitters, I imagine," he replied. He may not have been articulate, but at least he wasn't a snitch. She gave a curt nod.

"Very good. Show her to her room," she said. She addressed me directly, her voice cold and stiff.

"I'll be along shortly to give you your first treatment, young lady," she said. I tried not to show it outwardly, but the way she said that made me feel nervous. No one had yet bothered to explain to me what kind of treatments I would be getting at this rehab place. I just hoped it wouldn't be group therapy. Group therapy sessions always just turned in a trauma competition without fail. Sam took me gently by the elbow and showed me to a tiny little room with just enough space for a twin bed and a nightstand. As he closed the door behind him, I heard a lock slide into place. Here I was, locked up yet again. I sat on the tiny bed and tried not to cry.

I waited for what felt like hours, but I had no way of telling how much time had passed. Finally, Deborah unlocked the door and instructed me to follow her. She led me to a communal bathroom and told me to shower. I was grateful for the chance to get clean. It had been well over a day since I had last showered and I probably stank to high heaven. The water was hot and soothing, but when I tried to linger under the calming spray, Deborah barked at me to wrap it up. When I emerged from the shower stall wrapped in a towel, I saw that the clothes I had arrived in were gone. In their place was a neatly folded nightgown with an adult diaper sitting on top. I eyed it warily, unsure why they would think I would need that.

"I can go to the bathroom on my own, you know," I said, gesturing towards the diaper. Deborah only shook her head and tutted.

"Potties are for big girls. Babies wear diapers. Put on your diaper, little one. It's time to feed you and put you to bed," she said. I stared at her, speechless. I thought for a moment that she must be joking or might be having some fit, but she only matched my gaze with another icy stare.

"Are you going to be a good girl and do as Nanny says or shall I call Sam in to do it for you?" Deborah asked. The thought of that giant, ogre of a man putting a diaper on me was too embarrassing even to consider. Reluctantly, I complied and slid the diaper on, feeling like an absolute fool. The diaper made me feel puffy and bloated, and I was grateful that the oversized, shapeless nightgown hid that I was wearing it. I felt utterly ridiculous and was very glad that there was no one to see my shame.

Deborah led me back to my room. While I was showering, someone had brought in a tray with a baby bottle and a pacifier. Deborah sat on my bed and patted her lap, indicating that I should sit. I hesitated in the doorway, briefly wondering if I had gotten high somehow, like some flashback.

"This is weird. What's happening?" I asked, my eyes shifting nervously around the room. Deborah rolled her eyes and sighed. Her voice took on a lilting, patient tone as though she were speaking to a small child.

"You have been a very naughty girl, that is why the judge sent you to us. It's not your fault, of course, you didn't have a Nanny like me to raise you to be a good girl. Doctor Franken has designed a treatment for little girls like you so that we can get all those mean, nasty thoughts out of your head that are making you be naughty and help you to be the good girl that we know that you can be," she explained. She smiled at me expectantly as though that cleared everything up. I stared at her for a moment, still thoroughly confused. Then, I suddenly remembered an article I saw while waiting at the health clinic about age regression therapy. I didn't read it, of course, but it was full of hilarious pictures of grown adults in diapers, sucking on pacifiers. And now it was happening to me of all the rotten luck. I hesitated near the doorway and considered my options: throw a tantrum and end up being force-fed by Sam the orderly or play along until it was time to be released from this weird place. I decided the second choice seemed like the easiest, at least for now, and sat uneasily on Deborah's lap.

How bad could it be, after all? I thought to myself. She was a large woman, not obese but tall and broad. *They certainly found the right woman for the job.* I thought as she drew me to her bosom and placed the bottle between my lips. I felt engulfed in her arms, which was strangely calming. I suckled tentatively. I tasted the protein shake, vanilla bean. As soon as I started drinking it down, I realized how hungry I was and drank faster. It had been far too long since I had last eaten anything.

"That's a good girl," Deborah cooed. "What a hungry baby you are!" She began rocking me back and forth and humming a lullaby. I had expected to hate it, or at the very least to barely tolerate it, but to my surprise, it was incredibly soothing. My eyes began to grow heavy, and my suckling came slower and slower. I'm not sure if it was the exhaustion or if there was some sedative in that protein shake. Either way, I was drifting off to sleep in Nanny's warm embrace before I could even finish my bottle.

Chapter 3

I'm not sure how long I slept, but it was daylight when I woke up. I was still a bit groggy, but overall I felt much better after a good night's sleep. Someone had placed the pacifier in my mouth after I fell asleep and I spit it out, rolling my eyes. I stretched and shifted in the narrow twin bed to find that my diaper was moist and squishy between my legs. The smell of stale urine wafted up as I moved, verifying that I had wet my pants in the night. I groaned, burning with humiliation. I couldn't believe that I had peed my pants like a baby! They must have sedated me, that is the only way I could have wet myself without realizing it.

The lock slid open, and Deborah came right on in without knocking or even announcing herself. In my embarrassment, I quickly pulled the covers up to hide my puffy diaper, not wanting her to know that I had wet myself in the night. It was futile, however, as the very first thing that she did was to pull the covers right off of me and immediately begin feeling the front of my diaper. I blushed and turned my head toward the wall, sure that I was about to get a lecture of some kind.

"Oooh, it looks like somebody has a full diaper," she cooed.

"That's a good girl. It looks like I'll have to change you," she said. She began to hum a little tune as she reached into the nightstand and pulled out wipes, baby powder, and another diaper. I was confused. This was not quite the reaction I was expecting. She seemed pleased that I had dirtied my diaper for some reason.

"Change me?" I asked, shocked by her words.

"Of course. Babies can't clean themselves up; that's what they need Nannies for," she replied as though it was the most natural thing in the world.

Oh right, the whole age regression thing, that had sort of slipped my mind. I needed coffee, but something told me that wasn't going to be on the breakfast menu. I was willing to play along to some degree in the interest of speeding things along and possibly even getting released early, but having some strange woman be so involved in my bodily functions was a bridge too far.

"Look here -" I began, ready to give her an earful but the cheeky bitch just shoved the pacifier back into my mouth and got on with it. I sulked but decided once again that the consequences of putting up a fight were likely worse than just going along with it.

She pulled the soggy, soiled diaper away and began to clean me up with baby wipes. I would never have admitted it in a thousand years, but it felt very nice to have the stale, sticky urine cleaned away. The baby wipe was soft and sensual against my sensitive areas, and her perfunctory, efficient movements put me at ease. A little bit of powder, and before I knew it, I had a fresh, clean diaper on. This woman knew her way around a diaper change. I had to give her that.

"Now, who's ready for breakfast?" she said

her in her best baby voice. I screwed up my face into a grimace, ready to throw a tantrum. I was too hungry for another protein shake. I wanted real food, damn it. To my relief, Sam came in just then with a tray of oatmeal. Not my favorite breakfast, admittedly. I would have preferred a big greasy breakfast of bacon, eggs, and buttered toast. But, under the circumstances, I was just happy to have solid food. He was also dragging an oversized high chair behind him which Nanny took from him and began to set up.

"What is that?" I asked, looking at it uncertainly. Surely they didn't expect -

"Hush," Nanny cut off the thought before I could even finish it.

"Babies can't be expected to feed themselves, now can they?" She said.

"But -" I stopped short as Sam loomed over me, silently daring me to misbehave. My still sore ankle reminded me that I probably should not protest too much. He picked me up and put me in the chair, and Deborah put an adult-sized bib on me. She spoon-fed me oatmeal while cooing and babbling at me like I was a tiny baby. Thankfully, Sam did not stay to watch. He lumbered off to whatever it was that he did when he wasn't bullying young women into high chairs.

Despite my skepticism, I found myself surprised by my response. Being fed was a lot more fun than eating breakfast on my own, and I caught myself caught up in Deborah's choo-choo train game more than once. This age regression therapy was disarmingly powerful. The more that they treated me like a small child, the more normal and natural it felt to act like one.

After breakfast, Deborah announced that I was going to meet Doctor Franken today and I groaned inwardly. I'd had to talk to endless counselors and psychologists and everything in between during my time in the system. I never found it at all helpful. Still, I knew the rules of the game pretty well by now. Smile, play along, follow the rules, get released, rinse, repeat. Deborah made a big fuss out of finding a pink dress covered in ruffles for me to put on and even found ruffled socks and a shiny pair of mary janes shoes for me to wear. The dress was so ruffled that you couldn't even tell that I had a diaper on underneath. She brushed my hair into pigtails and topped it all off with a bow before standing back to admire her handiwork.

"The doctor is going to like you," she said with an odd twinkle in her eye. I didn't fully understand what she meant by that, but it did make me blush.

Chapter 4

I soon found myself in a chair just outside of the doctor's office, feeling somewhat nervous and more than a little silly. The outfit that Deborah had picked for me made me feel more like a Victorian doll than a grown woman. I sat on my hands and kicked my feet, a nervous habit I've had ever since I was a little girl. I hoped that this doctor was nice.

"Come in, Molly," beckoned a deep, masculine voice as if on cue.

I walked into the office slowly. Behind the large, wooden desk was a man both younger and more handsome than I would have expected. He was in his early to mid-thirties, perhaps, I've never been very good with ages. He had short brown hair and a well-groomed beard, neither of which showed any signs of gray. There was something comforting about him, something in the way his tweed suit crumpled and the way his wireframe sat at an odd angle on his handsome face that made him seem gentle and approachable. I didn't usually find beards attractive, but it suited him. Out of nowhere, I wondered if his beard would tickle if I kissed him. I blushed and tried to put the thought out of my mind.

He was writing something down as I walked in and his glance up at me turned into a double-take. His sleepy blue eyes suddenly took on a hungry look, taking me in from head to toe as though I were the most fantastic thing since the Grand Canyon. Deborah had been right. The doctor seemed to like me very much, indeed.

"Ms. Molly Banks," he said slowly, letting his pen fall to the desk. The sound seemed to bring him back to reality, and he regained his professional decorum. He cleared his throat and straightened his jacket, then gestured toward the chair opposite his desk.

"Please, sit," he said.

His eyes never left me as I crossed the room and lowered myself onto the chair. Never able to pass up an opportunity to flirt, I let my knees gape open just wide enough to make him wonder. He coughed again and messed around with the papers on his desk for a moment before he could manage to look me in the eyes.

"How are you getting on so far?" he asked, doing a medium job of keeping his voice steady.

"I guess I'm doing ok," I said in a small voice.

"It has been a weird day if I'm honest," I replied. He nodded sympathetically and smiled.

He has such a charming smile, I thought dreamily.

"I know that age regression therapy can seem a bit strange at first, but I promise you that if you keep an open mind, you will be astonished at how quickly you can make progress. How are you adjusting to your diaper?" He asked. I'd forgotten all about that for a moment. I blushed deeply and clamped my legs shut, suddenly feeling like an idiot for trying to flirt while wearing a diaper.

"Um ... " I stammered. He chuckled at my embarrassment, which only deepened my humiliation.

"Don't worry. That will take some adjusting to as well. I encourage you to use it as often as you can. In fact, for the first few days at least, it will be a requirement. It does help to put you in the correct mindset. And, on that note, after this initial consultation, you will no longer refer to me as Doctor Franken. From henceforth, you will call me 'Daddy.'" He waited and looked at me, expectantly.

"You want me to call you, Daddy? You can't be serious," I scowled at him.

"I am very serious, young lady, and you can wipe that pout off of your face right now. I allow no brattiness here. You see, I represent a father figure for my patients, something many of them lacked growing up. By bringing you into a regressed state of mind and providing you with that positive father figure while in that state, we hope to train away all of that naughty behavior you've been engaged in recently," he explained. I frowned but resisted the urge to argue, sensing that it would get me nowhere or worse.

"Ok, if you insist," I pouted.

"I do insist. Furthermore, you will refer to Nurse Roberts as 'Nanny,'" he added.

"Who, Deborah?" I asked, guessing that was who he meant.

"No, no," he wagged a finger, reproachfully, "Not Deborah. *Nanny.*"

"Right. Nanny," I said, playing along.

"And I am?" he leaned forward eagerly in his chair. I could almost taste how badly he needed to hear it. Something about that eagerness excited me. I looked down shyly at my lap before looking up at him through a veil of lashes.

"Daddy," I said the words so softly that I was almost speaking in a whisper. He nodded and closed his eyes, savoring it. I wondered if he reacted this was to all of his patients and thought sent a little stab of jealousy through me.

Careful, Molly. This is not a guy you need to be crushing on, I thought to myself.

"Good girl," he said, somewhat shakily.

"Now, that's enough grown-up talk. I

believe that Nanny has coloring books and juice waiting for you back in your room. Run along now," he said. I grinned to myself as I walked back to my room, thinking of how flustered he had gotten when I called him "Daddy." I knew how much that had turned him on, and I had no qualms about using that attraction to get what I wanted, an early release. I was so sure that I had him eating out of the palm of my hand, but I had no idea just how wrong I really was.

Chapter 5

"No, little girls go pee-pee in their diapers, not in the toilet!" Nanny cried exasperated. It was late that afternoon, and I was refusing to wet my diaper.

"Please, Nanny, I have to go so bad!" I hopped from foot to foot and squirmed, but the urge to urinate was uncomfortably strong no matter what I did.

"Then go in your diaper!" She crossed her arms and looked at me expectantly.

"Well?" She questioned. I burst into tears. I couldn't do it no matter how hard I tried. Nanny made an irritated noise and grabbed me by the hand, dragging me out of my room and down the hall. Some small part of me realized how ridiculous I must have looked: my bow was crooked, my face was red, and my eyes were swollen from crying. The rest of me couldn't care less, though. I was too upset at being in trouble.

After a few short days of coloring, storytime, and naptime, I was already in a deeply regressed state of mind. The cynical brat who had arrived at the Institute was gone. I truly wanted to be the good little girl they expected me to be. I couldn't get over this last hurdle. Nanny marched me straight into Daddy's office. Daddy put down the book he was reading at looked at us with a perplexed look on his face.

"What's going on here?" he asked, a hint of annoyance in his voice from the interruption.

"Well, go on and tell him," Nanny said firmly, giving me a gentle push towards Daddy's desk. I tried to get the words out without crying but failed.

"I can't pee in my diaper," I wailed and buried my face in my hands to hide my shame.

"Oh dear," I heard Nanny tutt quietly behind me. I could sense their disappointment, and it made me want to be swallowed up by the Earth and die.

"Molly," Daddy said gently.

"Look at me," he added. I brought my hands down just low enough to meet his gaze.

"I told you that you would have to use your diaper for the first few days, remember? If you don't go tinkle in your diaper, I'm afraid that you'll have to be punished. You don't want that, do you?" He asked. I shook my head silently, my bottom lip quivering.

"Good. Now be a brave girl for Daddy and use your diaper, ok?" His soothing voice said. I gave it one last shot, but no matter how I tried, not even a drop came out. Daddy sighed with disappointment.

"Okay, little one, if that's the way it's going to be. I want you to know that this will hurt me a lot more than it hurts you," he said. His eyes told me his words where true. Nanny led me over to his desk, my face still streaming with tears, wondering what he was going to do to me, fearing the worst. He pulled me onto his lap, face down, and pulled up my skirt. Before I even had a chance to react, he whacked my diapered bottom with his hand, very hard. I froze with fear and pain, too shocked to even cry. Over and over, he brought his hand firmly onto my rear end without mercy. Even though the padding of the diaper, every blow stung more than the last. The pain and humiliation were overwhelming, and, after the initial shock wore off, I began to sob. I sobbed and squirmed and kicked my legs but Daddy just held me tighter and didn't relent. He methodically covered every square inch of my bottom with blows. As much as it hurt, as much as I wanted him to stop, I couldn't help but notice that my body was also humming with arousal. That made me feel even more ashamed of myself, and I cried even harder. At last, I was so overwhelmed that I was finally able to pee.

Once it began, it all came flooding out of me, and I completely soaked my diaper. The spanking stopped, and Daddy patted the back of my diaper approvingly. He held me close, patting my puffing diaper and rocking me until I stopped crying.

"It's ok, sweetie," he would occasionally

mutter.

"Let it all out. Cry as much as you need to. Daddy is here. So is Nanny. You're ok. Everything is alright," his words were soothing, and his embrace was warm. I relaxed into him, forgetting all about the pain and the shame, enjoying the feeling of being held. I felt so safe there. When my sniffling finally stopped, he gave me one last firm squeeze on the butt before telling me to stand up. My legs were wobbly, but I managed to stay upright as he inspected me. He reached under my skirt and felt the puffy swell of my diaper, patting it with satisfaction. To be sure, he pulled on the elastic waistband and inspected me visually as well.

"Good girl," he muttered as he looked at me.

"You were such a good girl, taking your spanking so well. I'm very proud of you for using your diaper," he said. It was as if his eyes burned right into me and I couldn't help but feel proud of myself when he said those words, even though a small part of me was still mortified that I had just peed my pants. The doctor had worked up a light sweat from spanking me. He pulled a handkerchief from his jacket pocket and dabbed at his forehead as he regained his composure.

"Take her to get cleaned up," he instructed Nanny.

"And make sure she is properly shaved at once," he said before we left the room.

Chapter 6

To my surprise, Nanny didn't take me back to my room or to the communal showers, but rather to a private bathroom. It was considerably more beautiful, with a huge clawfoot bathtub, scented candles along the rim, and an assortment of bath toys waiting in a basket on the floor. Nanny drew some warm water, sprinkled in a few bubbles, and removed my pretty, ruffled dress and soggy diaper.

"Good girls get bubble baths," she cooed as she helped me in.

"And you've been a perfect girl," she added. Now that I had submitted to their wishes and peed in my diaper, she was as cheerful as the sunshine, humming a little tune as she scrubbed my body thoroughly. She gave me a few toys to play with as she washed my hair, and I lost myself in a cute little game of sink the ducky. The warm water was relaxing, and Nanny's fingers on my scalp felt like a lovely massage. She had me lean back as she poured bathwater over my hair, rinsing all the suds away until I was squeaky clean. All too soon, bath time was over, and Nanny had me on my bed with my legs in the air, ready to be shaved. She covered me with shaving cream and set about the task of shaving me, which she did with military precision. Her touch felt more maternal than sexual, and I relaxed into the pleasant sensations of having my vagina shaved by somebody else. I usually do the task myself, and it was only a few days overdue, so Nanny was able to make quick work of it. It was quite lovely to be pampered after such an emotionally draining day, almost like what I imagined a spa day would be like. With expert precision, Nanny applied the powder and a fresh diaper, giving me a little boop on the nose when she was done.

"I imagine that you're ready for bed little one," she said in a sweet voice as she pulled my nightgown down over my head.

"You have had a massive day today. Nanny

is very proud of you," she said, making me smile. Her words made me blush. It was barely dark outside, but she was right. I was exhausted! The thought of curling up against Nanny's bosom as she fed me a bottle sounded delightful. She had Sam bring in a fresh bottle and rocked me gently as I suckled on it. As I sucked it down, she told me a story about a pretty princess who was kidnapped by a mean old dragon and taken away to live in his evil kingdom. The good knight fought his way over treacherous mountains and dangerous deserts on his way to rescue her. I fell asleep somewhere between the dragon-slaying and true love's kiss.

***

Bill watched the woman go, her wet diaper making her ruffled dress puff out behind her. He normally didn't let his tendencies affect his job, but this young lady was having an unusual effect on him. She was so beautiful but also very vulnerable and eager to please. She had taken to the age regression therapy quicker than most and was already using her diaper.

That doesn't make her a little, Bill warned himself. *Don't get your hopes up,* he said to himself. Being a Daddy was hard sometimes. His job as a counselor was gratifying, and there were indeed similarities to the lifestyle, but it wasn't the same. He longed for a real relationship, a baby girl that he could call his very own. Most of the women he'd dated were varying levels of disinterested or disgusted by his affinity. On the rare occasions when he had met a woman who shared them, they had turned out to be incompatible in other areas. Bill sighed heavily, suddenly feeling very lonely. He wanted to take Molly home, dress her up in the prettiest dresses, buy her all the toys her heart desired, and snuggle up next to her every night.

You're dreaming. She's a patient. She isn't interested in you. She doesn't want you creeping on her. But the way she called him Daddy on her first day here, breathless and excited, wouldn't let him give up hope entirely. The memory made his cock throb. So too, did the recent events. It felt delicious to spank her and check her diaper. At that moment, he had done his best to maintain a clinical detachment. Now, alone, the memory was driving him wild. He got up and locked the door to his office. Sure that he wouldn't be disturbed, he kicked off his trousers, taking his erection in hand. In his mind's eye, he saw Molly kneeling before him clad only in a diaper and little white bows on her pigtails. She was playing with her nipples as she watched him stroke himself.

"Want some help with that, Daddy?" asked his fantasy.

"Yes, baby girl," she lovingly said. She wrapped her warm, soft lips around him, sucking him like a lollipop. He moaned as her little pink tongue worked its way up to his shaft. She gently cupped his balls and smiled up at him with the face of an angel.

"Cum for me, Daddy. Cum all over my face!" He obliged her, and she giggled as he showered her with his love.

That's better, he thought, feeling a bit more clear-headed.

You really shouldn't be thinking of a patient like that, anyway. He quickly cleaned up his mess and unlocked the door. Thoughts of Molly still lingered in his mind, however. He wasn't able to shake them, no matter how he tried to distract himself or tell himself that she was out of bounds.

The next day started much the same as all the others had, only this time when the smell of urine and the squishy diaper between my legs made it clear that I had wet my diaper again, I was relieved instead of ashamed, knowing how proud of me Daddy and Nanny would be. Sure enough, Nanny was full of praise for me when she saw how full my diaper had gotten overnight. She even gave me a strawberry sticker to play with as she cleaned me up and put a fresh, clean diaper on me. The soft material of the diaper rubbed against my freshly shaved vagina in the most exhilarating way. As a familiar tingle came over me, I thought back to the hungry way Daddy had looked at me, and the tingle only got stronger.

Nanny announced during breakfast that today's treatment would be just before lunch. I smiled and squirmed in my highchair, eager to find out what the doctor might have in store for me today. The morning seemed to drag on, but Nanny finally announced that it was time for my treatment. As I walked to Daddy's office, I began to feel a little bit nervous, remembering the day before. What if he spanked me again? It wasn't that painful, it had even stirred some pleasant feeling in me, but the thought of going through it still filled me with dread. What was it about it that scared me so? Then, it hit me. It was his anger that I feared, not the spanking itself. I didn't want to disappoint him. Daddy was waiting for me in the middle of his office. A fluffy purple blanket spread out at his feet. He looked very handsome in his tweed jacket and neatly trimmed beard. As he smiled at me, I felt my insides clench with excitement.

"Good morning, princess," he greeted me as I came in.

"Nanny tells me that you've been a very good girl for her this morning. I'm very proud of you," he said. I blushed and looked at the floor, overwhelmed by the emotions that he made me feel, but also embarrassed that his opinion carried so much weight with me. After so many years of cynically rebelling against authority, craving approval felt a bit strange. The doctor continued.

"You've made excellent progress in your regression. Today, I want you to go a little bit deeper. The deeper into regression we can take you, the more the positive messages will be able to implant into your subconscious. I thought we might start with some tummy time," his said, clapping his hands together.

"What the fuck is tummy time?" As soon as the word left my mouth, I knew I was in trouble. Daddy's eyes narrowed, and his voice grew cold.

"What did you just say?" he snapped. I gasped and covered my mouth with both hands, but it was already too late. I couldn't believe it. Here I was supposed to be putting myself in the mind frame of a little girl, and before I could stop myself, the dirtiest word of them all had come flying out of my mouth. Hot tears welled up behind my eyes. I honestly was a bad girl. Despite his tightly controlled exterior, his anger and disappointment were palpable.

"That is a no-no word! You know what happens now, little one?" I shook my head. My hands still clamped over my mouth.

"You're getting your mouth washed out with soap," he ordered. Before I could react, he was dragging me by the hand to his private washroom attached to his office. He turned the water on in the sink and pulled my hand away from my mouth. Squirting a tiny amount of hand soap onto his index finger, he turned to face me.

"Open," he commanded. I could already feel the stinging in my eyes and knew that tears wouldn't be far behind if he would just let me explain.

"Daddy, please -" Before I could get another word out, his finger was in my mouth. The soap tasted terrible, and he rubbed it all over my tongue and teeth.

"This will teach you never to talk like that again. That kind of filthy language does not belong in the mouth of little girls, do you hear me?" He barked. I nodded and burst into tears. His anger was too much for me to handle. At the sight of my tears, he softened a bit.

"Alright, little one, rinse out your mouth," he said. He held my hair back as I bent over the sink, cupping the water into my mouth and ordering me to spit it out until the taste of soap began to fade away. When I was done, he gently dried my red-splotchy face off with a hand towel. I must have been a sad sight indeed my swollen eyes and damp dress because he picked me up as though I weighed nothing at all and carried me back into his office. Still cradling me against his chest, he sat in one of the chairs and wrapped his arms around me tightly, burying his face in the top of my head with a sigh.

"I'm so sorry that I made you mad, Daddy," I said, rubbing my eyes.

"Do you forgive me?" I asked, my little voice quiet against his chest.

"Daddy isn't mad at you anymore, sweetheart. And I'm sorry that I had to punish you like that, but it's important for you to learn how to behave like a good little girl. It's my job to teach you right from wrong, and if I don't do that, I can't be a good Daddy to you. Do you understand?" He explained. I nodded and sniffled. He put his finger under my chin, gently raising my face to meet his own.

"Look at me, little one," he said. With big, watery eyes, I met his baby blue gaze.

"Of course, I forgive you. There is nothing that you could ever do that I couldn't forgive. I might have to punish you from time to time but don't ever think for even one minute that it means that you're not my princess anymore," he said. He pulled me close, and I closed my eyes, relaxing into his warm embrace. He petted my hair and kissed my forehead until my tears finally stopped.

"There's my brave girl," he said gently, wiping my nose with his handkerchief.

"Now, let me see you smile," he said.

I managed a tiny, shaky smile, but Daddy wasn't satisfied with that. He tickled my sides and underarms until I shook with laughter and squirmed to get away, the sound of my giggles filling his small office.

"That's better," he said and pulled me close to him once again. I could feel the hardness that had grown in his lap, and instinctively I squirmed against it. He inhaled sharply as my padded bottom made contact with his erection. I bit my lip, blushed, and looked away as if it were an accident.

"Well, I think that's enough time for today, little one," he said abruptly, standing up and walking me briskly to the door. He paused before closing the door behind him.

"You did very well today. I'm proud of you," he said.

Something about the way he said it, his voice warm and soft, made me tingle in my diaper again. I thought about how hard he had gotten when I giggled and squirmed in his lap. It was apparent that he wanted me, but he had cut our session short just when things were starting to get juicy. Had I done something wrong? On the other hand, he had said that he was proud of me just before I left, so that was confusing. I decided not to worry too much about and skipped down the hall back to my room where Nanny would be waiting with cookies and juice.

***

That evening, Bill couldn't manage to sleep no matter how hard he tried. He couldn't get Molly out of his head. It didn't matter how many times he masturbated, thoughts of her were never far behind.

This was more than just sexual attraction, he realized. He wanted to hold her, to talk to her, to protect her. A sweet thing like her needed protection. She should have someone watching over her, keeping her safe. Sadly, she had no one at all. She was all alone in the world, and it broke Bill's heart.

He sighed and turned over onto his side, punching his pillow to try to reshape it. He shouldn't be having these thoughts, he knew. He should be focused on her recovery, on getting her healthy, on helping her get over her past. Her life story read like a horror novel, losing her parents suddenly in a car crash at a very young age, passed from foster home to foster home, kicked out at eighteen when the government's money dried up. He cursed the sorry excuses for foster parents she had been subjected to. She deserved so much better. You would have never known that she had lived through so much just by talking to her.

How could someone who had lived through so much pain be so sweet? He thought.
Most patients lashed out in cruel ways during their recovery. It was only human nature. Molly, however, never had. Yes, she had thrown temper tantrums, but never once did he hear her say one cruel word to him or Nurse Roberts. Not only was she beautiful and vulnerable, but she was also sweet and submissive. She deserved to be cherished, to be somebody's baby girl.

Not mine, he thought, his heart aching.

Stop thinking of her like that. You're a professional. It didn't matter how many times he said it, thoughts of her ran through his mind unbidden.

I need a break, he thought.

I need a chance to clear my head, to get her off my mind. He decided that he would cancel her treatment tomorrow. It was better to fall one day behind on their progress than to risk doing something inappropriate. He flashed back to the moment earlier in the day when she had innocently brushed against his reaction and blushed.

What a pervert she must think I am! He couldn't shake the feeling that she was attracted to him as well. The way she looked at him seemed to hang on his every word. If that were true, it would only make things worse. He would never be able to resist her if she wanted him as well. He groaned and rolled over again. Yes, some space would be wise.

Chapter 8

That evening, I didn't go down when Nanny gave me a bottle like I usually did. I couldn't stop thinking about Daddy and the special tingles he gave me. As Nanny tiptoed out of the room, thinking I was asleep, I began to squirm in my fresh diaper, letting the silky material rub against me. With a glance at the door, I snaked my hand down the elastic band of my diaper. The light dusting of baby powder made my freshly shaved skin feel silky-smooth against my fingertips. As my fingers found my magic button, my eyes fluttered closed, and I thought of Daddy. His big, strong hands wrapped around me, holding me close. The way his pants bulged every time he saw me, the hungry look in his eyes. I knew that he wanted me, and it drove me crazy. Being desired was a powerful aphrodisiac for me, and his lust was setting me on fire. I reached under my frilly pink nightgown and groped my tiny breasts, pinching the pert pink buds until they stood rigidly at attention. I thought of all the cute nicknames he had for me, *princess* and *little one*, and how special they made me feel. In my mind, I could hear him telling me what a good girl I was and how proud he was of me, over and over, until I was shivering with pleasure. I hesitated before allowing myself to climax, however. Whenever I orgasmed, it made a huge mess, gushing out of me in waves. Usually, that wasn't a problem because my underwear wasn't being inspected every morning under usual circumstances. On the other hand, I desperately needed to relieve some tension if I had any hope of getting to sleep.

If I wet my diaper, Nanny will never notice, I suddenly realized. I smiled and went back to rubbing my magic button, imagining that it was Daddy's hands, not mine, guiding me gently but firmly to an earth-shattering orgasm. I bit my lip so as not to cry out and let it all come rushing out of me, flooding my diaper with my slick juices. For a long moment, all I could do was take shaky, rapid breaths, and try not to moan out loud. After a while, I came back to myself. Should I wait to see if I would wet my pants overnight? I decided it was best not to take the chance. Some things are better left private. I had a faint urge to go, and it took some coaxing to come out. I was still adjusting to using a diaper to pee, especially when lying down. Nanny assured me that with more practice, it would become more comfortable and easier, but I was still struggling. I bore down harder and managed a small sprinkle, adding to my already soggy diaper. It was a warm and soothing sensation, and before long, I was fast asleep.

Chapter 9

Nanny didn't notice anything unusual about my diaper the next morning, other than to remark that it seemed extra full. This earned me lots of praise and a banana sticker to add to my growing collection. I played with it gleefully as she cleaned me up and put a fresh, clean diaper on me.

All morning, I looked forward to my next treatment with the doctor, but Nanny never did take me. By the time lunch rolled by, I had begun to worry that I wouldn't see him that day, but I did my best to put the thought out of my head. When nap time came and went, I was feeling downright distraught. What had I done wrong? Did he hate me and never want to see me again? It may sound irrational, but in my regressed state of mind, it was the only possible explanation. I was a bad girl, and he didn't want to be my Daddy anymore. The thought put me in a terrible mood, and I refused to cooperate with Nanny on any front. I wouldn't color or sit still for storytime. I threw my afternoon snack on the floor. The age regression therapy had done its job very well, and I was no longer able to express my anger and frustration like an adult would. I was no longer capable of saying, "Nanny, I would like to see the doctor now, please. I think treatment would do me good." I could only throw my cheerios in the poor woman's face and hope that she somehow got the message.

"That's it!" she finally snapped. "I'm afraid I'm going to have to tell your Daddy on you, young lady!" she exclaimed. I froze with fear. I had wanted his attention so badly that I didn't think about what that would mean if it was in response to a tantrum. I immediately burst into tears. He would be so angry with me! Desperately, I begged and pleaded with Nanny not to tell on me. I promised to be a good girl and to go to bed early, anything to win my way back into her good graces. Nanny had no sympathy for me. I had successfully pushed her well beyond her limit. She dragged me right down the hallway and made me wait outside while she told Daddy every horrible thing that I had done to her that day. I sobbed and wailed as I waited, beyond caring who saw or heard me and what they might think. After a few minutes, Nanny stepped out and informed me that Daddy would like to see me in his office right away. I obeyed, tears still streaming down my face. Daddy watched silently as I crossed his office slowly; my vision still somewhat blurred. Once I was settled in a chair, he leaned down and gently wiped my face with his handkerchief before commanding me to blow my nose into it. His tone told me that he was in no mood for backtalk, so I complied. He wiped my nose gingerly before folding up his hanky into a neat square and placing it back in his jacket pocket.

"Now I want you to stop this nonsense right away. Nanny says that you have been terrorizing her all day. What could have possibly gotten into you?" he asked sternly.

"You were doing so well," he added. I tried to find the words to explain that I was confused and afraid and lonely but failed. Another wave of tears threatened to come up, but I managed to barely hold them back with a trembling lip. I looked at him with watery eyes, silently begging him not to be angry with me. Daddy sighed and took off his glasses.

"I know this has been a big week for you, little one. You've had a lot to adjust to, right?" He said. I nodded and sniffed. He squatted down so that we were eye-level.

"Listen to me, sweetheart. You can't go around throwing temper tantrums every time you don't get what you want. This is a very critical time for your therapy. We have reached the stage in your development where you need to learn to ask for what you want," he explained. I looked at him, wide-eyed, his words not registering in my regressed state of mind.

"I need you to use your words like a big girl," he elaborated, his velvety voice was like a warm blanket wrapped around me, keeping me safe.

"What made you so upset today pumpkin?" He asked. He put his hand on my knee and looked at me with those deep blue eyes and it finally all came rushing out of me.

"I wanted to see you, but Nanny didn't bring me down for my treatment, and I got scared that you didn't want to see me and maybe I did something wrong, and you didn't like me anymore," I blurted out. All of this was between great heaving sobs, but I managed to get it all out before dissolving into a total hysterical mess. Daddy picked me up and sat with me in his lap, holding me while I cried.

"There, there," he muttered occasionally as I wept. I completely soaked his tweed jacket with my tears, but at no point did he chastise me or act disgusted. He only held me and stroked my hair, letting me cry as much as I wanted to. Finally, I managed to stop long enough to ask, "A-are you going top-punish me?" He sighed and kissed my forehead, his soft, warm lips lingering on my skin.

"No, little one, I think this one is Daddy's

fault," he said. I looked up at him, my head still resting on his shoulder, my brows knitted together in confusion. He smiled down at me and brushed his fingers lightly over my moist cheek, wiping away the tears that still lingered there.

"I should have had an appointment with you today. You are here because you need help. It wasn't fair of me to cancel your treatment just because of my feelings. I'm very sorry. Do you forgive me?" I nodded at him, unable to speak. His fingers brushed over my lips, and for one breathless moment, I thought, hoped, that he might kiss me. The moment passed, however, and he didn't kiss me, much to my disappointment. Instead, he sighed sadly before leading me over to the bookshelf next to his desk. The bottom shelves were filled with picture books and puzzles.

"I think I owe you a little one-on-one time. Pick something out, and we'll do it together," he said. He rested his hand on my shoulder and looked down at me with a warm smile. I suddenly felt like the whole world was glowing, especially me. I considered the options for a moment, then decided that a puzzled would probably take the longest, therefore giving me more time with Daddy. I found the puzzle with the most amount of pieces and handed it to him with a smile. Daddy patiently helped me put the puzzle together. I got a great deal of enjoyment of pretending not to know how to fit it together and the gentle way. Daddy would show me how to do it correctly. Something about the soft way he spoke to me and the affection in his eyes made my heart blossom open. I wanted nothing more than for the afternoon to go on and on forever. Of course, the time passed all too quickly. Daddy announced that he had another appointment to get ready for and I tried not to pout, even though I wanted to.

"I do have something for you before you go, however," he said. He walked over to his desk and pulled something out of the drawer. As he brought it closer, I saw that it was a small silver box. He handed it to me.

"Go on, open it," he encouraged. I looked at

his shining face for a moment before I gently pried the lid open. Inside, nestled in velvet lining, was a silver pacifier with "Daddy's Girl" engraved into it. I picked it up reverently to find that it was a functioning pacifier with a rubber tip and everything. I put it hastily in my mouth and grinned.

"You look beautiful, honey," he said. Then, he leaned down and kissed my pacifier.

"Run along now, Daddy will see you tomorrow," he said as I left. My heart was all aflutter. He had kissed me! Well, sort of. As I walked into the lobby, I saw another young lady, all dressed in ribbons and bows. When she saw my pacifier, she screwed up her face in anger.

Eat your heart out, I thought, somewhat ungenerously, and skipped happily back to my room.

***

As Molly left, Bill finally admitted that something had to be done. She was pretty clearly reciprocating his feelings. He knew that he wouldn't be able to resist her charms forever, not when he knew that she wanted him as well. He also knew that nothing could happen between them while she was under his care. He went to Molly's file and opened it, seeking out the name of the judge who had sentenced her. Surely, there was a reasonable solution to be found.

Chapter 10

The next several days passed uneventfully. I stopped counting the days until my release and began to enjoy my time at the Institute. Daddy said I was making excellent progress in my treatments, and I had the sticker collection to prove it. In my sessions, I slowly worked my way up in age, relearning important developmental markers that I had missed the first time around. I learned manners for the very first time, as well as the importance of being kind to others. Growing up in a dog-eat-dog kind of environment, this was a whole new world for me.

One day, Nanny announced that Daddy had a special surprise for me. A herd of butterflies instantly flooded my stomach. He had not outwardly shown any attraction to me in our recent sessions, but I knew it was still there. Every day I waited and hoped that today would be the day that he cracked and swept me off my feet, but it never happened. I tried looking as adorable and irresistible as I could, but still nothing.

What if today is the day? I wondered before pushing the thought out of my mind. Best not to get your hopes up in matters of romance as I had learned the hard way. Almost every crush I had ever had culminated in a half-drunk hump in the back of somebody's car.

Nanny had laid out some clothes for me, jeans and a beautiful blouse, very different from the frills and bows she usually dressed me in. Big girl clothes, as I had come to think of them. As I put them on, I began to feel closer to myself than I had felt in weeks. At the same time, I knew that I was different, healthier, and more confident. It felt good.

"My little girl is growing up," Nanny said as she watched me dress, dabbing a tear from her eye. I almost laughed at what I thought was a corny joke when I noticed that both the tears and the emotions were real.

"Oh Nanny," I said, quickly crossing the

room for a hug.

"I'll always be your little girl," I said, almost involuntarily. I meant it, too. When I first arrived, she had seemed so cold and stern, but now I thought of her as the grandmother I'd never had. Embarrassed by the show of emotion, I stepped back and looked into the small mirror hanging above my bed.

"How do I look?" I asked, unable to see below my shoulders in the small mirror.

"Beautiful," Nanny said, tearing up again, "Absolutely beautiful." This time I did laugh, hoping to cheer her up a bit.

"Ha! You have to say that, you're my Nanny," I said playfully. She managed a weak, watery smile before shooing me off to my appointment.

Rather than waiting for me in his office, as he usually did, Daddy was waiting for me in the lobby with his coat in hand. He was twirling his car keys on his finger and rocking back and forth on his heels. I wondered what had made him so happy.

"Hello, pumpkin," he greeted me with a happy smile.

"I thought we might go out for some ice cream, what do you say?" He asked with his handsome grin. I was so overcome with happiness that I couldn't say anything. I could only jump for joy and squeal with delight. Daddy threw his head back and laughed.

"I'll take that as a 'yes,'" he said and offered me his arm. I took it with a smile, and he led me outside to his car. It was the first time I had been outside in weeks. The bright sun made me squint a bit, but I was happy to be out in it nonetheless. The parking lot that had once seemed so dinky to me now seemed alive with flowering trees and singing birds. I even saw a couple of squirrels playing in the grass which I excitedly pointed out to Daddy. I wasn't sure if it was the oncoming spring or a change in my outlook, but everything looked so fresh to me suddenly, more alive. As we drove to the ice cream shop, I chatted happily about everything I saw out of the passenger side window and all the things I couldn't wait to do when I was done with treatment. The age regression had brought me out of my shell, and I no longer second-guessed every word out of my mouth, worrying if people would suddenly stop liking me. Daddy had assured me and reassured me on many occasions that I was a smart and funny young woman and that the world was lucky to hear as many of my thoughts as possible. I was so grateful to him for everything that he had done for me. We pulled into the ice cream store, and I excitedly grabbed for the handle, ready to bound out of the car, but Daddy put a hand on my arm to stop me.

"No, wait here a moment," he said kindly but firmly. We may have left the facility, but it was clear who was still in charge, something I found both comforting and thrilling. He got out and walked over to my side of the car, opening the door and extending his hand to me to help me out. I took it, somewhat breathlessly, feeling like the most pampered princess in all the land. The way he put his hand on the small of my back as he opened the door of the shop, guiding me inside, almost made me swoon. Once inside, I had some trouble picking a flavor. There were so many choices! Daddy let me try as many samples as I wanted, patiently allowing me to narrow down the options until I finally settled on a double scoop of chocolate ripple fudge on a waffle cone. Daddy only got a single scoop of plain chocolate. We found a quiet corner of the shop where we could sit and eat our ice cream in private.

"Thank you for the ice cream, Daddy," I said. It had been a long time since anyone had bought me anything, even something as simple as an ice cream cone.

"You can call me Bill if you want," he said.

"You know ... since we're not at the facility right now and all," he said.

"Oh," I said, slowly, not sure how I felt about that.

"Well, do you mind if I still call you, Daddy?" I asked, smiling as his face lit up.

"Not at all. I rather like it, actually," he

replied. He blushed a little when he said that and suddenly, we were no longer doctor and patient, we were just Bill and Molly, sharing an ice cream cone on a lovely day out. I liked seeing him blush. It was kind of nice to think that I might make him get butterflies in his tummy the same way that he did to me.

"Cool," I said with a grin.

"I like it too," he replied. We ate our ice cream in contented silence for a moment. It was nice to be with someone without feeling the need to continually impress them or entertain them.

"There was a reason I wanted to get you out of the office today. I have some fantastic news," he said after a time.

"Oh!" I said excitedly, my mind racing. I tried not to fidget or squirm in my seat, so I nodded encouragingly instead.

"What is it?" I curiously asked.

"I've spoken to the judge about you. We are both very impressed by the progress you have made, and we both feel that you were the product of unfortunate circumstances. I told him that you deserve a second chance, and he agreed. The judge has agreed to release you early on probationary status," he said.

"Yay!" I squealed. At last, I had my freedom back. Then my joy quickly died. If I had gotten this news last week, I would have been ecstatic. All I had wanted since my arrival was an early release. Now, it dawned on me that it would mean leaving behind all the things I had come to love about the facility, including Daddy and Nanny. *No wonder Nanny was so emotional earlier,* I realized, caught somewhat off guard by the heartache that the thought inspired. I wasn't so sure that I was ready to leave them behind.

"What's wrong?" asked Daddy, putting his comfortingly large hand over mine, sensing the sudden shift in my mood.

"Well, technically, I'm kind of homeless. I don't have anywhere to go," I admitted. I was more than a little embarrassed, feeling like a total loser.

"I was going to mention, and no pressure or

anything, of course. But I do have a spare room you could stay in until you find a place to stay," he said. He almost winced when he said it. He seemed so nervous that I would say no. When I squealed and danced in my chair, he perked back up again. God, he was just the cutest thing.

"Thank you, thank you, thank you," I gushed.

"I promise, I'll be a perfect roommate, and I swear not to overstay my welcome," I quickly added.

"Oh, I'm not worried about that," he said, giving my hand another firm squeeze. We went back to the institute to get my things. I didn't have many possessions, just a few changes of clothes. Nanny tearfully told me that she had added a few additional outfits for me as she handed me a duffle bag packed to overflowing. At the sight of it, I started tearing up as well, and soon we were hugging one another and blubbering. Bill tried awkwardly but gently to comfort us both.

"There, there. You're only moving a few

miles up the road, Molly. We can have Nanny over for dinner any time you both like. Won't that be nice?" He offered. It was a comforting thought. Nanny wiped my face with a hanky and sent me off with a kiss on the forehead. Bill wrapped his arm around my shoulder as we walked to the car, which lifted my spirits tremendously. Soon, I was buckled into the passenger seat of Daddy's car, holding his hand as we drove out of the gates of the Institute and towards our new life together.

Chapter 11

Bill lived in a small ranch style house. The interior was sparsely decorated, but the whole place was obsessively neat. There was a couch and a TV in the living room and a table in the kitchen and not much else. He showed me to the guest room, which had a futon hastily stashed in the corner and a small nightstand. It was pretty similar to my room at the Institute.

"We can fix it up however you like," he said, putting the duffle bag down on the futon.

"I'll take you wherever you like this weekend to get decorations or and anything else you'd like. Sorry about the futon. It was the best I could get on short notice," he said.

He went out and bought that specifically for me, I thought and blushed deeply.

"I love it," I said and smiled at him, hoping that he would know how sincere I was. Maybe some people would turn their noses up at a brand-new futon, but after a lifetime of sharing beds with foster siblings and, more recently, couch surfing, it was wonderful to have a space of my very own. His face lit up, and he took my hand in his, warm and strong.

"Really? I want you to be comfortable here. Maybe, in time, you will come to think of this as your home," he said. The thought filled me with such warmth that all I could do was grin at him and blush again. We looked at each other for a moment, hand in hand. Was this the moment when he would finally kiss me? He lifted my hand and kissed the back of it, tenderly, while continuing to look into my eyes. I felt my breath catch as his lips touched me, a surge of adrenaline flooding my body. Taking that as an invitation, he pulled me closer and cupped my face with his hand. His body was warm against mine, and I melted into him, my eyes fluttering closed.

"Molly," he whispered. Slowly, he pressed his lips to mine. He kissed me softly, gently at first, waiting for me to blossom open for him before deepening the kiss. As our tongues met, a shock of electricity sent shivers all over my body. All of the longing, all of the aching for him that had been bubbling just under the surface since we met suddenly came rushing to the surface. I made a soft noise of pleasure and ran my fingers through his silky, brown hair. I was ready to rip my clothes off and give myself to him then and there, but he didn't seem to be in any hurry. He explored my mouth slowly, savoring every detail. He broke off the kiss abruptly and smiled at me. I stifled a whimper of longing and neediness, wanting more.

"Well, I'll let you get unpacked. Think you'll be ready for dinner soon?" He asked. I felt hazy like I was in a dream, but I managed to nod and say "yes" and smiled as though every fiber of my being weren't on fire. He kissed me lightly on the forehead and left, closing the door softly behind him. I stood there as if in a daze, burning for him more than ever.

I emerged sometime later, having recovered my

wits and unpacked my bags. In addition to some extra clothes, I had discovered that Nanny had snuck some extra toys into my bag and it had taken some time to rank them and find them homes befitting of that rank. As I came into the hall, I was greeted by the most delicious smell. I followed my nose to the kitchen to find the table was already set, complete with candlelight. Bill was still moving things around in pots and pans, but already the aroma was delicious.

"Hey, princess," he greeted me with a smile. I blushed, pleased that he still used his special names with me.

"You have perfect timing. Dinner is almost ready, go ahead, and have a seat," he said.

"What's for dinner?" I asked as he pulled out a chair for me to sit in. I was a bit overwhelmed by all the attention, but I didn't want to show it in case he stopped. Overwhelming or not, I was eating it up.

"Chicken parmigiana," he said, turning back to the stove.

"I hope you like cheese!" He exclaimed.

"I sure do! Smells delicious," I said enthusiastically. I watched him cook for a moment, impressed at his skill. I could barely make macaroni without burning it. How could a man like that still be single? He had his place, a steady job, and was incredibly good looking. I felt so lucky at that moment, a handsome man cooking for me and a place to call home.

And it's just getting started. I thought as he brought over two plates. He tied a napkin around me like a bib and cut my meal up into little pieces, reminding me to let it cool before tucking into his plate. It was quiet as we ate, something that would have bothered me in the past, but tonight it felt comfortable. Just being around him put him at ease. I got full rather quickly, but I kept eating anyway because it was so delicious! I honestly couldn't remember the last time someone cooked for me, but it had to have been when I was still a kid. Eventually, he slowed down as well, clearly reaching his limits.

"Don't feel as though you have to clean your entire plate, princess?" he said with a wink.

"This is a heavy meal, even for a big guy like me," he said. He patted his belly and winked at me again, making me laugh. I put down my fork, admitting defeat. He was right. The meal was deceptively filling.

"I wanted to talk to you about something," he said, taking my hand from across the table.

"Since we're going to be living together for a while, I feel like I should be as honest with you as possible. You see, I don't just engage in age regression for my job. I also like to engage in age play as a lifestyle as well," he said. He paused as if giving me time to be shocked but of course, I wasn't. I had known this about him from the very beginning.

Did he think he was subtle? I stifled a giggle, not wanting to give him some a complex, and nodded encouragingly.

"Go on," I said.

"I like to nurture and protect; it's just in my

nature. It always has been. I don't know why I am this way, but I am, and there is no changing that. Being a Daddy lets me express that side of myself. It has been difficult, especially in terms of finding a woman who can tolerate it. I have yet to meet one who can. But today, at the ice cream store, you said that you would like to keep calling me Daddy. Did you mean it?" He paused and looked at me almost hopefully.

"I did! I love calling you Daddy," I nodded enthusiastically.

"Do you think you'd like to keep being little as well? Not all the time, just when you are in the mood," he asked, making me tilt my head from side to side. I considered it for a moment and realized that it had become a part of me. I loved being little.

"I could keep my sticker collection?" I asked, making him laughed and kissed my hand.

"Yes, you can keep your sticker collection. You can have anything you like, baby girl. Assuming that you want to be my baby girl, that is," he said with a smirk. It was my turn to laugh.

The thought of being his filled me with such joy that all I could do is let it spill out of me in ripples.

"Yes, I want that very much," I replied gleefully. He stood and picked me up from my chair, consuming me in a hungry kiss as he held me close.

"Oh, baby," he whispered against my lips.

"My sweet girl," he whispered into the kiss. He carried me to his room and gently laid me down on his bed, my hair fanning around me as he slowly settled his weight on top of me. He stared at me, wide-eyed, as he traced my lips and cheekbones with his fingertips, handling me delicately as though I were some rare work of art.

"You are so beautiful," he whispered.

"Inside and out. I can't believe how lucky I am. I can't get enough of you," he said. Again, he captured my mouth with his. This time the kiss was deep, his tongue insisting on dominance. I happily submitted, allowing him to explore my mouth, my neck, my breasts. He frantically pulled my shirt up, taking a nipple into his mouth and nibbling it lightly. I moaned and ran my fingers through his soft hair as he teased me with his lips, tongue, and teeth. He stopped just long enough to take my clothes off.

"Arms up," he commanded breathlessly and as soon as I obeyed, my shirt was gone. As he unzipped my pants, he saw that I was still wearing my diaper, and he breathed in sharply.

"Baby girl," he exclaimed before placing a gentle kiss just below my belly button.

"You are so perfect," he said. I blushed slightly as his words but inside, I glowed with pride. He peeled my pants off and took a moment to admire me as I lay there in only my diaper. His eyes drank me in as he began to remove his clothing as well. Underneath that tweed suit was a surprisingly toned body. Light brown hair sprinkled his chest and trailed down his washboard abs. Everything about him was so incredibly sexy. As he took his pants off, I noticed that just the sight of me was enough to bring him to full-mast. My diaper was the last to go, and we were finally both fully naked. He settled back on top of me, his hardness nestled between my thighs. I was already slick with desire, and my arousal made me bolder than I usually am. I ran my hand down his well-muscled back and over the swell of his firm buttocks, enjoying his body and the fiery desire that it awoke within me. His hands explored my body as well, traveling down the curve of my hips, up the length of my thigh, until he reached my dripping slit.

"Oh, my sweet girl," he moaned into my neck.

"You are so wet," he moaned. He parted my folds with his fingers, seeking out my slick pearl. As he found it, I dug my nails into his back and moaned uncontrollably.

"Oh, Daddy!" I shivered as rubbed my button.

"That's right, sweet one. Let Daddy take care of this little pussy of yours," he said. He lowered himself, trailing kisses down my chest and stomach. He inhaled my scent deeply before his tongue traced the edges of my sopping pussy. As his tongue found my clit, I nearly screamed.

"Daddy, that feels so good!" He moaned against my slit as he bathed me with tender caresses. As he devoured me completely, I thrashed my head against the pillow and knew that I wouldn't last long against this onslaught of pleasure. He pressed a finger against my opening and plunged it in. His tongue was warm and gentle, and his finger was firm and persistent, and before long, orgasmic waves were building up, threatening to crash all over me. He continued nudging me toward sweet release until I could take it no more. I kicked my legs against the bed, ready to burst.

"Mmm, you taste so sweet. Cum for me, sweet girl," he moaned. His hot breath against my aching pussy felt like heaven. With one final burst of ecstasy, my climax overtook me. I shuddered and screamed, gripping Bill's hair and drenching his face. He sighed with satisfaction and grinned up at me as I collapsed against the covers, still twitching and moaning, the occasional aftershock washing over me. He wiped his face on the sheets before repositioning himself. He kissed me deeply; his tongue still heavy with my sweet juices.

"Good girl," he sighed, taking his rigid cock in his hand.

"Is this still ok, baby girl?" He said, slowing down and looking me in the eye. I bit my bottom lip and playfully thought for a moment before giggling and nodding. I like that I know I could have said no. It was my favorite thing about him that I knew I was safe with him. He rubbed his hard cock against my swollen clit, chuckling at how it made me jump before tracing it down my slick labia. I could feel his cock begin to press into me, stretching me open. I opened my legs wider, allowing him to plunge into me. He was so hard, and I was still very sensitive from my orgasm, and so I shuddered as he took me. He claimed me with his thick cock, affirming that I belonged to him. He grabbed my ass, holding me against him for a moment, savoring the sensation of being buried to the hilt inside of me, before thrusting into me again. Slowly, he parted me with his hardness, filling me up over and over.

"That's it, baby," he cried out.

"You're doing so good," he added. I moaned and grabbed his ass, pulling him deeper inside of me, craving more, craving everything he wanted to give to me. He felt better than anything I had ever experienced, seeming to know all the right spots to hit and, even better, made sure to hit them with every stroke.

"Oh, god! Fuck me!" I exclaimed. I didn't normally say such dirty things during sex but just then felt like a wild woman, and I wanted nothing more than to be his slut. His and his alone. My words seemed to drive him wild because he began to fuck me with abandon, as though he had finally unleashed the animal within. I ran my nails down his back and buttocks as he pounded into me, overwhelmed with pleasure. Over and over, his thrusts came faster and faster, his hands grabbed at my flesh, gripped my buttocks, my thighs, my hips. His hands twisted into my hair, yanking my head back as he drove himself furiously into me, fast and hard.

"Is that what you wanted, princess? You like it when Daddy fucks you hard?" He groaned.

"Yes, Daddy. Yes! Yes!" I screamed. I was too lost in my pleasure to be articulate. Never before had I experienced such passion, such heat in a lover. I only wanted him to fuck me harder, faster, to never stop fucking me. His velvety voice was now ragged with lust as he growled and groaned with every penetration.

"Oh, my sweet baby. You're taking it like such a good girl. You feel so good around my cock. You are mine, mine, mine..." He groaned. He was so warm and hard inside of me, and I never wanted the night to end. I didn't have a care in the world, at that moment. All that mattered was that I was his and he was mine.

"You are so warm, my precious. So tight, so greedy for my cock," he said. At his deliciously sinful words, I clench tighter around him, causing him to shiver. I had never heard anyone talk like that before and it excited me. I could already feel another climax begin to build as his thick hard cock sent waves of intense pleasure throughout my entire being. My moans grew louder, and I thrashed my head from side to side, entirely overwhelmed by ecstasy. I tightened my thighs around him and held on as he guided me expertly to my second orgasm of the night. I let myself go completely, screaming and squirming underneath him as the most powerful orgasm I had ever had ripped its way through me.

As I quaked beneath him, I could feel him being pushed over the edge right along with me, his rhythm suddenly faltering as he cried out "baby girl!" and gripped my hair. I felt his warm seed coating my insides as he unleashed himself within me. He collapsed onto my breasts with a sigh, but I could still feel him pulsing inside of me. At last, the waves subsided, and we were left clinging to one another, breathless. He rested his forehead against mine, his arms wrapped tightly around me, still hard inside me. I felt utterly sated, content, and happy even. We lay like that for several minutes, catching our breath and exchanging tender kisses. Eventually, he rolled off me, lying flat on his back next to me, and pulled me to his chest. I let my fingers toy with his chest hair, not quite sure what to say.

"You've made quite the mess there, baby girl," he said, pointing to the large wet spot my multiple orgasms created.

"I think Daddy needs to give you a bath," he laughed.

Chapter 12

Bill held his hand under the faucet, checking the temperature of the running water before nodding that it was a safe temperature for his princess. He had filled the tub with bubbles and lit several scented candles, giving the small bathroom a dreamy, romantic atmosphere. Satisfied, he turned off the water and held out his hand for me.

"Ok, sweetheart. Let's get you clean. It's almost bedtime," he said. I took his hand and let him guide me into the tub. I lowered myself into the hot water, allowing the warmth to relax my muscles. I leaned back and closed my eyes happier than I had ever been at that moment.

"Feel good, little one?" Bill asked, his hand kneading the tense muscles of my neck.

"So good," I murmured. I slid further down into the hot water as he cupped his hands and began to wet my hair. The warm bubbles running down my scalp made me shiver with pleasure. As he began to work the shampoo in my hair, it felt amazing. His fingers were firm but sensual against my scalp. It felt so much sexier than when Nanny had done it for me all those times. I moaned and leaned my head back, not wanting him to miss a single inch. He grabbed a cup from the side of the tub and rinsed my hair until it was immaculate. He began to run a loofah over my body, slowly. He scrubbed my nipples, making me squirm a bit at the sensation, despite the thorough fucking I had just received. I sighed and arched my back, leaning into his strokes with the loofah.

"My baby girl is so greedy," he said playfully.

"Are you already feeling tingly again?" He asked. I giggled and nodded, feeling a bit shy suddenly. He moved his eyes up and down my body, obviously enjoying the sight. He moved the loofah down to my stomach, tickling me with its soft touch. I giggled but didn't pull away. He stroked my face lightly as he let the loofah trail lightly over my labia, making me squirm. Teasing me, he moved the loofah down to my feet, tickling the bottoms with a wicked grin. This time I can't help but jerk my foot back, squealing with laughter as water sloshed over the side.

"Oh, I think I've found the sweet spot!" he said with devilish delight. He moves menacingly toward my other foot, making me squeal "no," my giggles echoing off the bathroom tile.

"No? That's not the sweet spot? Hmm, I'd better keep searching then," he teased. He dropped the loofah and slid his fingers lightly over my soapy calves, stopping to tickle my knees.

"Is that the sweet spot?" He teased.

"Nope," I giggled.

"Are you sure?" He screwed his face up comically, feigning doubt.

"Keep going," I said, hiding my grin behind my hands. He shrugged and ran his hands up my thighs. At last, he finds my pussy under the warm water and lightly traces my folds before gently parting me. I melt at his touch and moan softly as his fingertip finds my clit.

"Oooh," he said.

"There it is. Is that better, pumpkin?" He questioned. I nod and bite my lip, my hand seeking out my breasts. I play with my nipples as he runs his finger slowly over my button, watching me writhe and fondle myself with wide-eyed fascination.

"Looks like we still need to work on using your words," he said firmly.

"I asked you if that feels better," he said slightly more sternly.

"That feels so much better, Daddy," I said breathlessly. His commanding tone and methodical stimulation were intoxicating.

"Good girl," he said, never taking his eyes off my hands as they continued to play with my tits. He was still naked, kneeling by the tub with a bath mat to cushion his knees. I noticed that his cock was already back at full-mast, and I longed to taste it.

"Daddy," I said squirming. I looked pointedly at his erection, too shy to say it.

"What is it, baby girl?" He flicked my clit deviously, knowing that it would distract me further from being able to verbalize. He followed my line of sight, grabbing his massive erection with his free hand.

"Whatever could be the matter?" He asked, concern in his voice. I watched, mesmerized, as he slowly stroked his member while simultaneously stroking my pussy.

"I want … I want," I still couldn't get the words out. I had never asked for anything that I wanted before, sexually speaking. Usually, the guy just got himself off, and that was that. While I found the idea of saying those sexy words arousing, I couldn't quite get them out.

"What is it that you want, sweetheart?" He repositioned himself so that he brought that juicy cock closer.

"You can have anything you want. You have to ask," he gently said. I reached out to touch it, but he only swatted my hand away lightly before resuming his hypnotizing stroking.

"Come on, baby girl. Tell Daddy what you want," Bill lovingly said. I licked my lips and swallowed, screwing up my courage.

"Daddy, can I please s-suck your c-c-cock?" I stuttered a bit, but I managed to get it out. He sighed with pleasure at the sound of my words.

"Yes, baby girl. Of course, you can," he said, stroking my hair. He brought his cock to my lips, stroking my cheek lovingly. He pulled his hand from my pussy and replaced it with my own, leaving both of his hands-free to pet my hair as I took him gently into my mouth. At first, I only suckled the tip, savoring him. His cock still tasted of our combined flavors, and I moaned against his shaft. The slight vibration made him gasp softly.

"Good girl. You're doing so good," he said. He began to thrust in and out of my mouth slowly, testing my limits. I opened my mouth wider to take him deeper and twirled my finger around my slick pearl. As he thrusts deeper and deeper into my throat, I moan encouragingly, bobbing my head in the same rhythm. He threw his head back and moaned, resting his hand lightly on the back of my head, subtly encouraging me to take him even deeper. I worked his shaft down my throat until I felt myself gag lightly.

"That's it, kitten, choke on Daddy's cock," he said. I had never enjoyed deepthroating before, but something about the way he held my face tenderly contrasted with the dominant way he was inching his way down my throat made my pussy ache. I made a soft noise of pleasure as I rubbed my aching clit and tried to fit even more of him down my throat. I choked harder, and tears sprung to my eyes. He pulled back quickly, his face suddenly full of concern.

"Are you ok, sweetie? Did I hurt you?" He asked.

"I'm ok, Daddy. No, you didn't hurt me," I said. I opened my mouth to continue sucking him off, but he hesitates.

"We don't have to keep going if you don't want to," he said. I smiled up at him reassuringly.

"I want to," I said, reaching for his cock with

my tongue.

"What did we say about asking for what we want?" His tone had shifted from concerned to playful, and he tapped his cock lightly against my tongue, giving me just a little taste.

"Please, may I choke on your cock some more Daddy?" I blushed deeply at my own words. I sounded so dirty! Daddy was thrilled to hear me talking dirty because he thrust into my mouth, filling my throat with his cock once more.

"Well, since you asked so nicely, little one," he grunted and pushed his cock as deep as it would go.

"Good girl, just a little deeper," he moaned. I choked and sputtered a little, drool dripping from my lips. As he pulled out slowly, more drool spilled out onto my chin and chest.

"Daddy's little drooly baby," he chuckled and wiped my chin clean. I opened my mouth to receive him once more, but he shook his head.

"Stand up," he ordered. I obeyed him instantly, water cascading off of my naked body.

He kissed me, pulling me close. The air was chilly on my wet skin, but his body was warm against mine, so I nestled closer against him, shivering. He grabbed a towel and wrapped it around me, helping me out of the bathtub. He dried me off, running the soft towel up and down my nude body, admiring every inch, and squeezed the water out of my hair with the terry cloth. Once dry, he stood back and took me in, his hand absentmindedly grabbing his cock as he drank me in with his eyes.

"Turn around," he commanded. I could practically feel his eyes burning into me as I stood there, silent and motionless, awaiting his next command.

"Walk to the counter," he commanded. I tiptoed across the tile, aware of both the slippery floor beneath my feet as well as how my backside might look to him, wanting it to look as perky as possible. I stop when I reach the counter and wait once more. He doesn't say anything for a moment, and I wonder if he is still stroking his cock, but I resist the temptation to look, know it will only earn me a spanking — nude, this time, with no thick diaper padding to protect me from his sharp blows.

"Bend over," he said, his voice getting thicker and lower from arousal. I put my hands on the sink for balance and bend at the hips, pointing my bottom in his direction. I hear him pad over on bare feet across the tile until he is standing directly behind me. Still, he watches me quietly. At last, I feel his hand on my bottom, running his hand over my silky smooth skin.

"You are so perfect, baby girl," he whispered. I feel his cock pressing between my ass cheeks, sliding slowly between them as he softly sighed. He kept sliding down until he found my slick opening, still wet and eager for him.

"Oh, you are Daddy's perfect slutty girl," he said. He pressed his cock against my entrance but didn't enter me. I whimpered, burning with desire and yearning for him to take me again.

"What's wrong, princess?" he pressed his

finger against my clit, sending a jolt of pleasure through me.

"Did you forget how to use your words again?" He questioned. I moaned and gritted my teeth, having grown slightly bashful once again. I strained towards his cock, but he stopped me with a firm, painful slap against my rear end. I jerked away from the pain, but he took me by the hips and pulled me against him once more.

"You are going to have to learn how to ask for my cock like a good little slut, is that understood?" He explained. To accentuate his point, he spanked me again, very hard. I winced and whimpered, unable to ignore how the pain made my pussy get even wetter. I pushed aside my embarrassment and found my words at last.

"I want you to fuck me," I said, blushing deeply.

"I know you do, sweetheart. That's because you are Daddy's sweet little slut. Aren't you?" He asked. I nodded, but it wasn't good enough. *Smack.* Another jolt of pain and desire went through me as he slapped my bare ass.

"Tell me. Use your words," he growled.

"I'm Daddy's sweet little slut!" I cried out on the verge of tears. I was overwhelmed by pain, longing, and humiliation but far above all of that was the desperate desire to please him. He penetrated me but only slightly, not yet ready to give me my reward.

"That's right pumpkin. You are mine. Aren't you?" He asked.

"Yes, Daddy. I'm yours. I'm all yours. Please fuck me with your big hard cock. Please fuck me like a dirty little slut," I moaned as I felt him. The words came flooding out of me, begging him for sweet release. With one thrust, he finally gave me what I had been craving. He hammered into me, giving me the fucking I had begged for. His thick cock was hard as a rod inside of me, making me scream with every thrust. He put my hand on my pussy, guiding it to rub my clit as he pounded into me.

"Good little sluts cum when they are told to.

Think you can do that, my princess? Think you can cum for Daddy?" He asked as I squealed with ecstasy as I rubbed my nub.

"Yes, Daddy. I can cum for you," I panted. I was already close; his cock and my finger combined had me building toward yet another climax.

"Not until I tell you to, ok, pumpkin?" He lovingly instructed.

"Ok, Daddy. I'll try it," I said. I hoped that I could wait, but his cock felt so good inside of me, I knew that it was going to be difficult. He dug his fingers into my hips, pulling me back to meet his every thrust.

"Oh, you're so tight, baby girl! So tight and so wet. Oh, you're going to make Daddy cum!" He groaned. I could feel him getting harder inside of me, his pace quickening. I knew I only had to hold on for a few moments longer.

"Cum for me!" he commanded at last. I moaned with sweet relief, letting my climax wash over me. Together we cried out, his hand finding mine on the counter as he pumped me full of cum for the second time that night.

"Good girl," he peppered the back of my neck with breathless kisses before gently withdrawing from me.

"You are such a good girl," he added, looking at my body. He toweled off my legs where our juices had coated my thighs before tossing the towel onto the floor to soak up the small puddle there. He lifted me and carried me back to his bed, lowering me gently onto the mattress. He curled up next to me, holding me close and burying his face in my hair. He caressed my body lovingly, letting his hands wander freely over my naked skin. Occasionally, he squeezed me tightly, making me squeal and giggle. Mostly, though, we just lied there in silence, enjoying the feeling of our naked bodies entwined with one another.

"Where's your pacifier?" he asked after a long time, a hint of sleepiness in his voice.

"In my duffle bag," I murmured, noticing that I was beginning to drift away as well.

"Wait here," he said, kissing my forehead and getting up. The bed felt big and cold without him, I noticed, so I got under the covers and waiting as he had instructed. I heard him in the bathroom, letting the water out of the tub and cleaning up the mess we had made. Then, I heard the clattering of dishes coming from the kitchen, and the refrigerator door open once or twice. Finally, he came back into the room carrying my pacifier and a fresh diaper for me. He leaned over me, gingerly placing the pacifier in my mouth and sealed it with a kiss.

"All ready for bed, little one?" He asked, already knowing the answer.

"Yes, Daddy," I said, the pacifier making my words lisp just a bit. He grinned and pinched my cheek lightly.

"Such a cutie. Ok, let's get your diaper on!" He said and pulled the covers back and had me scoot my bottom to the edge of the bed and put my legs up in the air. He took his time putting the diaper on me, savoring the process. Once on, he patted the front of it with a twinkle in his eye.

"You look so beautiful, princess," he said, reaching out and stroking my cheek affectionately. For the first time in my life, I felt beautiful. The way he looked at me like I was a precious jewel filled me with such pride. I was proud to be his. His baby girl.

"Would you like to stay in Daddy's room tonight, sweetheart?" He asked, my sleepy face lit up.

"Can I?" I gasped in happy bliss. He chuckled.

"Of course you can!" He exclaimed. He walked over to his closet and pulled out a teddy bear. I sat up and clapped my hands as he gave it to me.

"I've been saving this, waiting for someone special to give it to. I've finally found her," he said. He kissed my forehead and then my pacifier again.

"My special girl," he said. Bill turned off the lights and joined me under the covers, pulling me close. I nestled my heavily padded bottom against him and closed my eyes, thoroughly content. I clutched my teddy bear close, feeling like the luckiest girl in the world.

"Goodnight baby girl," he whispered against my neck.

"Goodnight Daddy," I said, already drifting off to sleep.

Chapter 13

In the morning, I awoke to find that he was already up. I found a t-shirt in the closet and put it on. It was comically large, hanging almost to my knees, but it would serve for the moment. Groggily, I shuffled into the kitchen to find him making pancakes, as bright-eyed and bushy-tailed as if he had been awake for hours already.

"Good morning, sleepyhead," he chirped and kissing me on the forehead.

"Thought you were going to sleep all day," he playfully teased. He winked at me and patted the front of my diaper.

"Do you need changing?" He asked. He pulled the elastic out as he asked, visually checking my front to see that it was dry.

"No. I'm sorry, Daddy," I said and blushed.

"Well, that's no surprise. I made you squirt so many times last night you didn't have anything left!" He laughed. Having expected to be chastised,

I was caught somewhat off guard. He must have noticed my quizzical expression because he put down the spatula and pulled me close for a hug.

"You can wet your diaper, or not, anytime you choose, ok? If you feel like using the potty like a big girl, that's ok. If you'd rather have Daddy change you, that's ok too. Understood?" He said, looking me directly in my eye.

"Understood," I say, smiling. He patted my puffy rear.

"Good girl. Now, who's ready for some pancakes? I made yours with Mickey Mouse ears and chocolate chips for the eyes!" He exclaimed. We chatted excitedly as we ate our breakfast and drank our coffee, planning what we would do that day. Bill suggested that after breakfast, we should relax on the couch and watch a little T.V for a while. Then, we could go for a walk and have a bit of lunch.

"And later, maybe we could go get you some more permanent furniture for your room," he said as he blushed and suddenly seemed bashful.

"Or, for your apartment or whatever," he said quickly. I suppressed a laugh. He was so cute when he got like this, bashful and insecure. It was amazing to me how he could be so dominant and self-assured in the bedroom, yet act so nervous when it came to matters of the heart. As if he weren't completely perfect in every way.

"I think I'll be staying here for a while if that's ok with you?" He grinned at me, his shoulders dropping in relief.

"Yes! I was hoping that you would. I don't want to pressure you or make you feel trapped in any way. It's important to me that you are here because you want to be," he exclaimed, nodding enthusiastically.

"I want to be here," I said quickly, hoping that he would believe me.

"I want to be your baby girl more than anything," I said, eating my pancakes.

"I'm so happy to hear you say that," he said, kissing my forehead.

We cleaned up and set up camp on the couch. I have no idea what show he put on because we were so wrapped up in making out that I didn't pay it any attention. We never did make it out for that walk, either. This time when we made love, it was slow and sweet. He kissed me deeply as I rode him on the couch and afterward we cuddled, whispering and giggling together until cuddling turned to fucking once again. We enjoyed a simple lunch of sandwiches and sliced apples, deciding that we would try to find a chest of drawers for my room first so I would have somewhere to put all of my things.

"Not that I have many things," I said somewhat sadly.

"You will," he said, bucking up my chin.

"You can have anything you want. You know that," he said in a more serious voice than the one he usually used. We finally got dressed sometime after lunch. I was amused to see that his weekend attire was jeans and a t-shirt. I don't what I expected, exactly, I had just gotten so used to seeing him in tweed. I put on a t-shirt and a skirt. It seemed to amuse Daddy to reach under my diaper and squeeze my diaper.

We found a furniture store that would deliver. As we were about to go in, Bill realized that he had forgotten his wallet in the car.

"You go ahead, I'll catch up," he said, kissing me on the forehead and jogging back in the direction where we had parked. As I walked toward the entrance, I noticed a guy hanging around the cars. He was the kind of guy the old me would have been desperate to impress, saggy pants, stained tank top, drenched in cheap body spray. The sight of him brought back unpleasant memories of standing in parking lots just like this one, acting as a lookout for douchebags just like him as they tried to jimmy the locks of cars, looking for loose change and whatever they could steal from the gloveboxes.

"Hey little mama, how you doing?" he

sneered at me suggestively as I walked by, quickening my pace. I would have been putty in this guy's hand last month. Now, I only wanted to get away from him, but he followed me.

"Hey, I'm talking to you," he said, raising his voice, angry at being ignored. I only waved vaguely in his direction and kept walking, hoping that he would leave me alone. His pace slowed, but he couldn't resist taking one last shot at me.

"You ugly anyway, you dumb bitch," he yelled. I heard a commotion behind me, and I turned around just in time to see Bill decking the guy in the face. The douchebag went down like a sack of potatoes, and Bill stood over him, his fist still clenched.

"Go get in the car, baby girl," he said, handing me the keys. I took them from him hurriedly and made a beeline for the car. I got behind the wheel in case we needed to make a hasty retreat and took deep breaths, trying to calm myself.

I set down a bowl of ice on the kitchen on the kitchen table and put Bill's hand into it. He had banged it up pretty badly on that guy's face, and he was starting to feel it. It had been a somewhat tense ride home, but he assured me that he was ok and that nothing was broken, only bruised. I just wasn't sure if it was the unpleasantness of what had just happened that made him so quiet or something else. I sat beside him and decided that if he wasn't going to talk then maybe I should.

"Thank you, by the way. You know, for defending my honor and all," I said. He chuckled at that, the first smile I had seen him crack in a couple of hours.

"I didn't scare you?" he asked.

"Is that what's been bothering you? No, sweetheart. You didn't scare me. You were my knight in shining armor," I replied. He was visibly relieved.

"I'm so glad. I don't normally act like that. I'm not violent by nature. It's just when I heard him speaking to you like that and the way he was following you, I just, I lost it. Promise you weren't scared?" He asked again.

"He scared me. You were my hero. In fact," I got up and moved to his lap, wrapping my arms around his neck.

"It was more than a little sexy. The way you swooped in like some cowboy," I said. I kissed his nose, his forehead, his cheek. He sighed and wrapped his uninjured arm around me.

"Oh yeah?" He asked with a sideward smirk.

"Big time. No one has ever stood up for me before," I said nodding.

"You deserve it," he said, pulling my face down for a kiss.

"You deserve everything in the world. You're my baby girl, now, and no one will ever hurt you as long as I'm around. Understood?" He said.

"Understood," I repeated. He made me feel so safe and loved, more than I had ever thought possible. I was already longing for him again, despite the crazy amount of sex we'd had since I arrived yesterday afternoon.

Who knew happiness would be such an aphrodisiac? I thought as he pulled me down for another kiss, so full of heat and passion that I knew that he was feeling it too. He gripped my bottom, pulling me against his already hard cock.

"You drive me crazy, little one," he whispered, moaning as I ground my pussy against him.

"You are so sexy, so sweet," he continued covering my cheek in kisses. He trailed off and kissed my neck, brushing my hair back with the hand that just been in the ice, making me squeal and jump.

"Daddy, that's cold," I complained and poked my lip out. He laughed.

"Sorry! I forgot!" He laughed. I rubbed his injured hand between mine, bringing the blood back to it, and kissed the bruised spot.

"There, now it's all better!" I declared.

"That's right, pumpkin," he said, nuzzling my neck.

"You are the best nurse," he said. He licked my throat, nibbling and kissing me there until I was desperately squirming in his lap.

"What's wrong, sweetie?" he teased.

"You got ants in your pants or something?" He laughed.

"I've got the tingles," I admitted, putting his hand on the front of my diaper, showing him exactly where the offending tingles were.

"Oh, I guess we'll have to take care of that," he said. He put his hands under my bottom and lifted me onto the table. Sitting in the chair, he spread my legs open and reached under my skirt and pulled down my diaper.

"Show Daddy again where the tingles are," he said, looking at me expectantly. His eyes followed my every movement as I parted my folds for him to see.

"Hmm, yes I think I see the problem now. This pussy is dripping wet," he smirked.

"Oh, no!" I said, feeling both silly and horny, a new combination for me.

"What do we do?!" I giggled.

"You'll have to listen very carefully and do exactly what I say, ok, princess?" Bill said.

"Ok, Daddy! What should I do first?" I asked.

"First, I want you to touch your clit," he instructed. I put my finger on my button as he watched me closely.

"Good girl. Now move it around in a circle," he continued to instruct. I did as he said, twirling my finger and moaning softly as it sent ripples of excitement all through my body.

"Like that, Daddy?" I asked.

"Slower, baby girl. I don't want you to cum until I say so, ok?" He said. I slowed my pace as he had instructed. The slower pace amplified every sensation, making my entire body feel electric.

"I won't. I'll be a good girl," I moaned.

"I know you will. You're Daddy's good girl," he said. He watched with silent fascination as I fingered my pearl and moaned softly.

"Stop," he said suddenly. I took my finger

off but whimpered and stuck out my lip. Daddy spanked the inside of my thigh.

"What's all that pouting, little one? If Daddy tells you to stop, you stop. Understood?" He said making me know that I better stop pouting.

"Yes, I understand," I said, trying not to show my disappointment on my face.

"Good girl. Now, put your finger inside that tight little pussy," he said. I sank my finger into my eager hole, my thigh still stinging. Eagerly, I sought out the sweet spot under his watchful eye, sighing with pleasure once I found it.

"Does that feel good, pumpkin?" He asked, already knowing the answer.

"Yes, Daddy. That feels so good," I replied. His eyes twinkled.

"Good. Now, move it in and out. Remember to go slow," he said. I loved having his gaze upon me as I pleasured myself. I went as slow as I could, moving my finger in and out of my aching pussy, noticing how it ached all the more for the hungry look he was giving me. He looked ready to devour me, but he only watched.

"Now, use two fingers," he said, continuing to tease me with his slow instructions. I swallowed, never having put two in before. *Smack.* My hesitation cost me as he brought his hand down on my other thigh, leaving behind a red mark.

"What did I say about doing what Daddy tell you?" He commanded.

"I'm sorry, Daddy," I said, biting my bottom lip, not wanting to disappoint him.

"Don't be sorry. Just do what I tell you," he replied. I nod and put a second finger inside, inching it in slowly. I feel myself stretch open to accommodate it and it feels so deliciously good that I let my head roll back and moan.

"See pumpkin? Daddy knows what's best for you and that slutty little pussy of yours. Isn't that right?" He questioned.

"Yes, Daddy knows best," I said, my fingers buried in my slick canal. Another whack on my thigh and Daddy's voice turned authoritative.

"Am I going to have to get my belt? Daddy knows best about what?" He asked. His control over me was intoxicatingly erotic.

"What's good for me and my slutty little pussy," I gasp. The stinging pain that lingered on my thigh heightened the pleasure I was giving myself.

"Daddy?" I ask, my voice taking on a high pitched, pleading quality.

"Yes, pumpkin?" He said, running his hands over my thighs. He never took his eyes off my fingers as the disappeared and reappeared from my dripping pussy.

"Can I cum? I need to cum. Pretty please?" I begged. I hoped that if I asked very nicely, he would grant my request, maybe even fuck me and let me cum on his big yummy cock.

"You are a perfect girl for asking first. But no," he said, making me almost whimper.
I tried very hard not to pout, knowing it would only earn me another spanking on my thigh. He stood from his chair and pulled his cock out.

"Daddy gets to go first, tonight," he said. He started stroking his cock, continuing to watch me finger my pussy. It was so tantalizing, seeing his cock so close but not being allowed to touch it, only being allowed to fuck myself slowly. I ached to feel his throbbing hardness inside, pounding me closer and closer to the edge.

"Stop," he barked, and I quickly pulled my fingers out, panting with desire. He smiled, stroking his cock faster.

"Good girl. You're such a good little slut for Daddy, aren't you?" He asked.

"Yes, I'm a good little slut for Daddy," I said. I blush as I say the words and my pussy begs for stimulation. I loved being dirty for him, how it only brought us closer together. It feels so good knowing that he isn't here for a quick fuck. No, he will settle for nothing less than owning me completely and ruining me for all other men.

"Pull your lips apart. Let me see my beautiful girl," he said. I spread my legs open wide and part my hairless pussy for him to see. I'm so wet that I glisten under the kitchen light.

"Oh, baby, you're so beautiful," he said, almost mesmerized by my body. I blush again. Never before has someone looked at me so intimately and with such raw passion. He strokes his cock furiously, his eyes glued to my pussy splayed out before him.

"I'm going to cum," he announced, positioning his cock over my pussy.

"Keeps those lips open, baby girl. My sweet, dirty girl," he groaned. With a loud grunt, he lets himself go, spraying my pussy, tummy, and tits with his cum. It felt so warm and gooey as it hit my flesh, and I felt as though he is marking me. The idea set my whole body on fire, loving how it felt to be his. He pushed his still hard cock into me, making my eyes roll back in my head.

"Do you want to cum on Daddy's cock?" he asked, putting my hand on my clit as he thrust into me.

"Yes! Can I please cum on your cock, Daddy?" I begged.

"Yes, baby girl," he said. He pumped into me, hard and fast, already familiar with the pace that drives me the wildest.

"Go ahead and make yourself cum," he said. I rubbed my clit, still slick with his jizz, as he split me open. Seconds later, my whole body was on fire as the climax came on me hard and fast. I quaked and screamed, totally lost in the ecstasy. I soaked him and the kitchen floor as I was taken by wave after wave. Finally, I was spent, and he chuckled approvingly.

"That was a big one!" He exclaimed. He scooped me up and took me to the bathroom to get cleaned up. Wetting a washcloth, he tenderly wiped me down, cleaning all the sweat and jizz off of me. Once I was all clean and dry, he picked me back up and carried me to the bedroom.

"You've had a long, hard day," he said as he lay me down on the covers.

"I think it's time for a nap," he added.

"That sounds nice," I agreed as he snuggled up next to me.

"Know any good lullabies?" I said, cuddling his arm.

"Just one," he whispered and began humming gently in my ear. The soothing sound worked like a charm, and I drifted off in his arms.

Chapter 14

Bill had some jello waiting for me when I woke up.

"Sex, sleep, and snacks? You certainly know how to keep a woman happy, don't you?" I tease, joining him on the couch.

"I hope so. That's the plan anyway," he said. He paused the video game he had been playing and wrapped his arm around my waist and pulled me close. I laid my head against his shoulder, wiping the sleep from my eyes.

"How are you feeling? I hope that jerk didn't upset you too much," he said, holding my face in his hands and looking me in the eye.

"I feel fine, honestly. Let's forget about him," I said.

"Good," he smiled.

"But, while we're on the subject of feelings, I want you to know that I've spoken with my colleague Dr. Saperstein and he is going to be taking over your therapy," he said. I pulled back a little, startled.

"You think I need therapy?" I gasped, a frown forming on my forehead.

"I think everyone needs therapy, said the therapist," he laughed.

"Seriously, though. We ended your treatment at the Institute early, and I want to make sure that it doesn't cause any unforeseen problems. A Daddy has to make sure his baby girl is completely healthy," he tapped my forehead lightly.

"Including up here," he said.

"Does he do age regression therapy like you do?" I smiled and conceded.

"No, but he is familiar with it. He is also familiar with age-play as a lifestyle so you can tell him anything and you don't have to be embarrassed," he said. I nodded, feeling better about the whole thing already.

"And seriously," he continued, cupping my face with his hands.

"Don't feel weird about being in therapy.

Everybody has stuff they have to work out," he said before he kissed me softly, then pressed the jello snack into my hand.

"Now be a good girl and eat your snack," he said.

"Ok, Daddy. Will you help me with the top?" I asked. He pulled the silver foil off the top, and I dug in my spoon.

"Thank you for taking such good care of me, Daddy," I said around a mouthful of orange jello.

"I'll always take care of you, baby girl," he said.

The rest of the weekend went well. We decided to shop online for furniture, not wanting to leave our little love nest. Daddy told me to pick out anything I wanted and not to worry about the price.

I spent all of Sunday afternoon in my little space. Daddy watched me color, play with my stuffies, and even read to me when it was nap time. I drew him funny pictures of him and Nanny which he put on the fridge, affixed with colorful magnets. He let me help him make dinner, explaining to me patiently all the steps, and why it was essential to follow each one, watching with pride as I tried to follow his instructions. I felt so relaxed in my little space, forgetting all about my grownup worries. I wish I had known about being a little earlier. It would have been a beautiful escape. When Sunday night rolled around, I found myself getting nervous about Daddy going to work Monday morning and leaving me at home all alone. At first, I didn't say anything, hoping that it would pass, but as we were getting ready for bed, he asked me about it directly.

"Do you think you'll be alright while I'm at work tomorrow, sweetheart?" I fidgeted nervously and looked at the floor, embarrassed by my anxiety.

"I don't know," I replied. He put down the pillow he had been fluffing and rushed over to put his arms around me. He cupped my face with my hands and forced my face up to look at him.

"What's wrong little one? No, don't look

away. What's bothering you?" He asked.

"I'm not sure, exactly. Just when I think about being here all alone tomorrow, I get a tight feeling in my chest," I said.

"Ok," he said slowly.

"Do you want me to call Dr. Saperstein and see if he can fit you in tomorrow," he said.

"No," I replied quickly.

"I don't want to make a bit deal about it. It will only make it worse," I said.

"Well, we don't want that," he said.

"Ok, how about this. You can text me anytime you want tomorrow. I won't always be able to write you back right away. I have patients to see. But you can write to me as often as you like and I promise to read them as soon as I can," he said. I thought about that, and it did sound a little better, knowing that I could contact him at any time.

"And," he said, pulling my teddy bear out from under the bed where it had fallen.

"Hamilton will be here to keep you

company," he added.

"Oh, is that his name?" I asked.

"Sure, didn't he tell you?" He asked before he addressed Hamilton directly.

"How rude of you, not introducing yourself," he said. I giggled, wondering how I had gotten so incredibly lucky to have found such a sweet and sexy man.

"Well," he continued chastising the bear.

"You had better be a lot more friendly to Molly tomorrow, Mr. Hamilton or you'll have me to answer to when I get home," he said. He handed the bear back to me and put his hands over its ears whispering.

"I'm so sorry he's not normally like that," he playfully said.

"You're so silly, Daddy!" I exclaimed.

"I sure am," he said as he pulled me close once more and kissed me lightly on the lips.

"Feeling a little bit braver about tomorrow?" He asked as he tucked me into bed.

"Yes, Daddy. I'll be brave," I replied as I fell

asleep.

I did well the first part of the day. Daddy made breakfast, just as he had all weekend. I watched him get dressed and sent him off to work with a kiss. T.V kept me distracted for the better part of the morning. Daddy texted once or twice to check-in, and I reported that everything was good so far. I made myself some lunch and cleaned up a little. Bill was pretty neat for a bachelor, however, so that didn't keep me very occupied for very long. The afternoon is when things got bad. Afternoons had always been hard for me. I get tired and cranky. I knew that I should try to take a nap, but I was too restless. I tried cuddling with my teddy bear, but it did not soothe me enough to drift off to sleep. I tried texting Daddy, but he was with a patient and didn't write me back. Eventually, I just sank onto the kitchen floor and cried, trying to figure out why I felt this way.

***

Bill was having a hard time concentrating on his staff meeting with Nurse Roberts. He knew Molly was having a difficult time at home, and it killed him that he couldn't be there for her. His phone vibrated on the desk repeatedly.

"Do you need to get that?" Deborah asked after the eighth text in a row.

"It's Molly," Bill said, picking up the phone.

"She's having a difficult time adjusting," he said.

"Poor dear," said Deborah. They had gotten close during Molly's time at the Institute. Bill's wasn't the only heart his baby girl had captured.

"I can't decide if I should take a personal day to be with her. I hate seeing her upset, but on the other hand, maybe she needs to learn a little more independence. What do you think I should do, Deborah?" He asked, feeling slightly lost.

"I think you should stay here and let me go check in on the poor girl," she replied, hoping he would agree, smiling when he nodded.

"Yes, that's the perfect compromise, I think. She shouldn't have to go through this alone. I'll text her and ask if she's up for company," he said. He had barely put the phone back down when he got his reply, and he chuckled as he read it.

"She says yes with fourteen exclamation marks. I'd say she's up for it," Bill said.

Chapter 15

I danced around the living room excitedly, eager to see Nanny again. It had only been a couple of days since I had seen her last but so much had happened since then. After what felt like hours but was probably only forty-five minutes, her car pulled into the driveway. I met her on the porch, and we hugged. I showed her around the house, proud of the small little changes I had already made to make the place feel a little less like a bachelor pad and a bit more like home. I poured us both a cup of coffee, and we sat at the small kitchen table to chat. She told me more about her life, and I learned that she had three grandkids that lived far away. Her husband had passed away many years back, and my heart ached for her, knowing all too well what it was like to lose someone much too soon.

"So, my dear," she said, bringing the conversation around to me.

"Bill tells me you're having a bit of a day," she said.

"I've had worse, I guess. I'm just not used to being alone. I've always had to share a space. I know that having a big house all to myself is a luxury, it's a luxury I've dreamed of all my life, but now that I have it, it's a lot to get used to. I don't know what to do with myself all day," I said, shrugging my shoulders. She nodded and took a sip of her hot drink, considering.

"Do you think you'll want to get a job?" She said, making me sighed.

"That kind of freaks me out, too. I've never been able to keep a job for very long. Always getting in fights with the customers," I honestly replied.

"Well, maybe not right now then. Sounds to me like you need a hobby. What do you like to do for fun?" She replied.

"I don't know. I've always just done whatever my friends wanted to do," I replied.

"Well, I think it's time to figure out what

Molly wants to do. Why don't you spend this week trying out different activities? Maybe you could take a few different classes a week until something feels right," I said.

"That's an excellent idea, Nanny!" I exclaim.

"But do you think Da - I mean Bill will pay for it? I don't have any money, you know," I said, a bit embarrassed. Nanny laughed, a deep belly laugh as though I had hit on comedy gold.

"Child, that man would give you anything and everything you could ever ask for, haven't you figured that out by now?" She questioned, making me blush.

"I know. I still get nervous asking for things sometimes," I replied. She nodded sympathetically.

"It will come with time. Just keep working at it. Remember, everything is a process," she said reassuringly. She downed the last of her coffee in one big gulp and stood to go.

"It was really lovely to see you again, my dear. I hope we do this again sometime soon," she said. We hugged, and she returned to work.

I spent the rest of the afternoon looking up pottery classes, yoga classes. You name it. Poor Daddy was going to have a whole list of activities to help me with when he got home. I giggled, thinking of how he would probably be delighted. Nanny was right, as always. Bill would help me in any way he could. I was so engrossed in what I was doing that I didn't even notice that it was almost time for Daddy to get home until he texted me.

Nanny says that you're feeling better. How was the rest of your afternoon? His message read.

Good. I am feeling better. I replied, smiling as I typed.

I have to stop by the store. I'll be home soon. XOXO. Came his last reply. I decided to put on a little makeup and a nice shirt, wanting to look nice when he came home. Just as I was putting on the finishing touches, I got another text.

I want you naked and kneeling by the front door in ten minutes. I felt a thrill go through me. Daddy had the best games. I stripped myself down and waited, already wet with excitement as I imagined the possibilities. When he came home, he had shopping bags in his hands. He noticed me, kneeling as per his instructions and smiled.

"Good girl," he said softly. He put down the bags and began slowly taking off his jacket and tie, watching my naked form as he did so. I stayed still, letting him claim me with his eyes, waiting for his next set of instructions.

"I missed you today, baby girl," he said as his shirt came off. He let his clothing fall carelessly to the floor.

"I missed you too, Daddy," I said, enjoying the view as he began taking his pants off.

"I'm glad you're home," I said.

"Me too, pumpkin," he replied. The boxers came off, and he stood before me in all his naked glory, his toned body moving as gracefully as a cat as he closed the small space between us.

"Open wide," he said, grasping his stiff cock. Eagerly, I opened my mouth, moaning at the taste of him as he slid his erection on my soft, wet tongue. "I've been thinking about this sweet little mouth all day," he explained. He grabbed the back of my head and eased his cock further down my throat. I looked up at him as he penetrated my mouth, dripping wet as I enjoyed the look of ecstasy on his chiseled face, knowing how much pleasure I was bringing him. He stroked my face as I choke on him, whispering encouragement as he gently pushed my limits.

"Keep that mouth open," he said as he pulled out. Drool dribbled down my chin and chest. He smiles down at, enjoying the sight.

"Did you like that, baby girl?" I nod, my mouth still open. He placed the head of his cock on my tongue.

"Do you want some more?" He asked, looking into my eyes.

"Uh-huh," I said. I nod again, my tongue caressing the sensitive underside of his cock. He pushed in, still testing my limits. I moaned as he slid down my throat. As his meaty erection cuts off my air supply, I notice how it intensifies every sensation. He began to pull back, but I grab his hips, reflexively pulling his back. He watches, fascinated, as I struggled to keep him down, not wanting to let go just yet. Who knew that I loved deepthroating so much?

I love deepthroating Daddy. Not just anyone. Only Daddy, I thought. He pulled out as I was beginning to get light-headed. He stroked his cock, watching me gasp for air.

"Are you ok, baby girl?" He asked, checking in to make sure that I still felt safe and comfortable. I nodded and swallowed.

"Yes, Daddy. I love sucking your cock," I said. I was glowing with pride as to how well I was using my words, not to mention what good slut I was for him. He looked at me with tenderness and heat in his eyes.

"Good girl," he purred.

"You're so sexy, little one. I love watching you suck me off. Ready for some more?" He asked, love, pouring from his eyes.

"Yes, please," I squeal and open my mouth wide. He sinks his cock in, even deeper than before. I relax into it, wanting to swallow him completely. In my eagerness, I go a little too far and choke, tears springing to my eyes.

"Go slow, baby girl. We'll get there," he reminded me. He set a hypnotizing pace, fucking my throat slowly but steadily. Even as his lust built, he still checked in with me regularly and caressed my face lovingly, telling me what a good girl I was. The more he praised me, the more my pussy tingled and dripped with desire. I kept my hands at my sides, however, knowing that he wouldn't like it if I touched myself without his permission. I swallowed his cock over and over, hoping that he would allow me to cum soon.

"Oh, baby, you're going to make Daddy cum. Do you want to swallow it?" Bill asked. The thought sent a thrill through me.

"Yes, Daddy. Please give me your cum. I want to swallow it all," I reply, trying to open my throat even more for him. My lips brushed against his cock as I spoke, and the sound of my sexy words made him go over the edge. I felt his cock pulse and opened my mouth eagerly. He shouted as he pumped my mouth full and I swallowed every bit of it down.

"Oh, baby," he said, coming back down to earth.

"You're such a good girl. I'm so proud of you," he said. He bent down and kissed me softly on the forehead.

"Daddy got you some new toys today, do you want to see?" He said, smiling at me. I nodded eagerly. My pussy was in dire need of attention, but it was hard not to get excited about new toys.

"Yes, gimme gimme," I squealed, and he laughed, bringing the shopping bags over to where I was still kneeling.

"Open this one first," he said, handing me one of the bags. I tore past the tissue paper to find a butt plug and some lube at the bottom. It was a pretty thing, something I didn't even know was possible, shiny silver with a sparkly pink jewel at the end. I picked it up to look at it and saw that it had "Daddy's girl" etched onto it. I blushed, not sure what to say. I had never used one of those before.

"Ok, now this one," he said, handing me the other bag. Inside I saw a vibrator. The box bragged about the many settings and attachments it offered. I blushed harder, wondering if Daddy was going to use this on me. My pussy was still aching, and I was desperate for relief.

"What do you think? Want to try them?" I felt a bit shy, never having used any props before, but I was also curious.

"Ok Daddy, let's try them," I said, biting my bottom lip.

"If you don't like them, you have to tell me. No lying," he said looking at me dead in the eye. His voice was firm, and my insides clenched, responding to his dominance.

"I promise, Daddy. No lying," I reply, my eyes going wide.

"Good girl," he said. He took the butt plug and lube from the bag.

"Bend over," he ordered, and I got onto all

fours. I heard him opening the lube and waited, unsure what to expect. I felt it press against my rear entrance, cold and slippery.

"How's that?" he asked.

"Okay so far," I said, holding my breath.

"Good. I'm going to push it in more. Let me know if I need to slow down," he instructed. He slid it in slowly. It wasn't very big and, to my surprise, it fit very easily inside of me. It felt nice once he worked it in. I had never been stimulated there before, and it made my pussy tingle. He stepped back to admire his handiwork.

"Oh, princess, you look so pretty. And you're sure it feels ok?" Bill asked.

"Yes, Daddy. I like it," I said. I could feel my heart racing with excitement.

"I'm glad. You can wear this anytime you like, okay pumpkin?" His fingers searched out my pussy, running along my labia and barely grazing my clit, causing me to twitch.

"Oh sweetie, you're so wet. Let's get you taken care of. Stay right there," he said. I remain on all fours as I listened to him take out the vibrator. He turned it on the lowest setting and pressed it against my pussy, causing me to moan and lean into it. It was the most delicious sensation I've ever experienced, sending waves of unspeakable pleasure all over my body.

"I think my baby likes that one," he chuckled, turning the vibrator off again. I moaned and yearned my hips backward, seeking the stimulation that was now gone.

"In a minute, sweetie. Let's you comfortable. Crawl to our bedroom. I wanna see that little tushie wiggle all down the hallway," he said, the smile on his face telling me all I needed to know. I started moving slowly, feeling somewhat drunk on desire. With every movement, I was made aware of the buttplug still inside of me, teasing me with its subtle sensations. I was also acutely aware of his eyes on my backside, loving the way he loved to look at me and how sexy it always made me feel.

Chapter 16

When I reached the bedroom, he picked me up and placed me on the bed face up.

"Daddy's in charge," he reminded me, spreading my legs.

"You are not allowed to touch yourself until I say so, understood," he added.

"I'll try, Daddy," I said, knowing how much of a challenge that will be.

"If you don't think you can resist, say so, and Daddy will tie your hands together for you. I know how horny my baby gets," he chuckled. I considered it for a moment and realized that he is right. I was so turned on. I would never be able to resist.

"You'd better tie me up," I said, eager to try yet another new fun game. He grabbed one of his ties and wrapped it around my wrists firmly; however, not so tight that it hurt my wrists.

"There. Now lie back and let Daddy take

over now," he said. I sighed happily as he turned the vibrator back on. Letting Daddy take charge felt so good and so right. I relaxed my legs open as he touched the vibrator to my clit. Again, my body was filled with the most delicious sensations, and I writhed on the bed. He had just begun, and already I was close to orgasming. My hands were restrained above my head, so I could only squirm and moan, entirely at his mercy.

"Oh, Daddy. I need - I need to cum. Please, can I cum?" I begged.

"Go ahead, kitten," he said. As soon as he said the words, my orgasm came gushing out of me. I screamed and quaked, the steady vibration sending powerful waves of pure ecstasy. The waves receded, but Daddy did not pull the vibrator away. He kept it right where it was, a devious twinkle in his eye.

"Daddy," I said, squirming away as I grew more sensitive.

"What are you doing?" I added.

"I told you, little one. Daddy is in charge

now. Stop squirming, or you'll get a spanking," he said. I settled back down or tried to anyway. I moaned and whined and squealed, the pleasure going between too much of a good thing and not enough. He began to manipulate my butt plug, sliding it in and out as I sputtered and squirmed. This time, however, I wasn't squirming away. The anal stimulation was sending me towards another climax, and I squirmed against the vibrator.

"Such a greedy baby. Are you already ready to cum again, sweet girl?" He said.

"Can I Daddy?" I begged, breathless, and horny.

"You can cum as many times as you like while Daddy is in charge, sweet one. I want to see just how many times I can make you squirt," he said. He bent over and nibbled my nippled, still manipulating my butt plug and I came again, even harder than the first time.

"Daddyyyy!" I cried out, thrashing my head from side to side as I let go. My breathing began to calm once more, but he still held the vibrator against my swollen clit. I kicked my legs and squealed.

"Oh, Daddy. I don't think I can anymore," I whined.

"You'd better try, pumpkin. Daddy isn't done with you yet," he said. I felt his hard cock press against my entrance, filling my sensitive pussy, making me scream with every inch. I was beyond all words, and all thought. He was in control, and I was his puppet. He thrust into me hard and fast, torturing me with pleasure from his cock, and the vibrator still pressed against my clit. I lost track of how many times I peaked. It seemed to go on forever. Finally, I felt his testicles tighten against me and heard him cry out my name. We climaxed together before collapsing into a sweaty, sticky pile. Movement seemed impossible for a very long time. I had turned entirely to jello. Finally, he disentangled himself from me and instructed me to stay where I was.

No problem there, I thought with a snicker. He returned with a sippy cup full of water and told me to drink every last job.

"Can't have my baby girl getting dehydrated," he said softly, taking the plastic cup from me and putting it on the bedside table. We cuddled and chatted. I told him about Nanny's suggestion and the classes I had found online. He was very excited about the idea and even wanted to take a couple of them with me. Our tummies began to rumble, so we finally emerged from the bedroom like two bears waking up from winter hibernation on the hunt for food.

Chapter 17

We found our clothes and got dressed, conceding that it was probably a bad idea to cook naked. I left my plug in, however, loving how it secretly marked me as his. He poured me a big glass of juice while he cooked and I chatted happily away, excited about my new classes. After we ate, he helped me get everything booked, once again telling me to not worry about the cost.

"I told you you could have anything you want and I meant it. I'm no millionaire, but I can take care of my baby girl. We'll have to schedule your classes around my work hours for now, but we should get you a nice, safe, reliable car pretty soon. Then, you can come and go as you please," he explained. He also suggested that a bit more structure in my life might help with my adjustment.

"What do you mean?" I asked. "Structure" was one of those words that teachers and guidance counselors liked to use but never took the time to explain.

"I think I should make a schedule for you, so you don't feel so lost all day. You mentioned that you didn't know what to do with yourself all day. This way, you'll know exactly what to do and at what time to do it," he said.

"So, you want to make a list of chores for me?" I whined. I scrunched up my nose, not exactly loving the thought. Then again, I supposed it was only fair, seeing as he was letting me live here rent-free. I should do something to give back.

"Chores might be a part of it, sure. But it will also be things like going to your classes and scheduled snack time and nap time. What do you think?" he asked.

"Let's try it!" I said. There was something about him taking control that completely, even of my mundane, everyday tasks, sent a thrill of arousal through me. I bit my lip as I watched him draw up a schedule, planning out my activities for the week. It was arousing, yes, but it also made me feel so safe and so loved, knowing that he cared about every detail of my life this intensely. No had ever shown me this much attention or affection, not since my parents died. Sometimes, I would wish that I could remember them better, but I was also incredibly grateful to have Bill. He made me feel like I finally had someone I could rely on.

"What do you think of that, pumpkin?" He handed the schedule to me, but I hardly looked at it. My trust in him was so complete that I glanced it over briefly and declared that it looked very nice indeed.

"Good. Try it out for a few days, and we'll see if we need to make any adjustments," he said. I got up to take care of the dishes, but he took the plate from my hand before I could even get it to the sink.

"Why don't you let Daddy take care of that while you put some fresh sheets on the bed?" He asked.

"What's wrong, don't trust me with sharp objects?" I teased. He laughed.

"I would trust you with anything, baby girl. You're the smartest and the bravest girl I know. It's just that Daddy likes to be in control, and that includes in the kitchen. If the dishes aren't loaded in just the right way well, it bothers me, that's all," he explained. I nodded.

"I get that. I get particular about my sticker collection sometimes," I said understandably.

After we had gotten our chores done, Daddy gave me a bubble bath, thoroughly sudsing me up from head to toe. As he ran the loofah over my pussy, I could feel myself reacting to his touch. Even after the countless climaxes, he had given me earlier. I was still so greedy for him. I could never get enough of how sexy and pampered he made me feel. The dominant energy came off of him in waves, and I always found it incredibly intoxicating.

"Looks like it's time for shaving, little one," he said. I instinctively grabbed for the razor, but he took it from me.

"Daddy is going to take care of that from now on, understood?" He said. He lathered my legs with shaving cream and ran the hard metal over my flesh, lightly and slowly. As he shaved me, his face took on that hungry look, and my fire for him grew even hotter.

This man is going to be the death of me, I thought happily, twisting so that he could shave all of my hard to reach places. The tub was too small for him to effectively shave my pussy, however, so he rinsed and dried me off and laid a towel down on the bathroom floor for me to lie on. He warmed the shaving cream between his hands before spreading it out over my mound and labia, letting his fingers linger over my clit. The foamy bubbles tingled and tickled the short hairs that had grown back in over the past few days, and I squirmed a little. He held the razor gently against my mound.

"Stay still, pumpkin. Daddy will have you taken care of in no time," he said. I held my legs open as he shaved me. The intense way he was staring at me and the way his breath started to come faster as he ran the sharp metal over my sensitive skin made it a much more erotic experience than when Nanny had done it for me. As he spread my lips to make sure he had done a thorough job, I heard him suck in air appreciatively at what he found.

"Oh sweetie, do you like when Daddy shaves your pussy? Just look at how wet you've gotten," he said. He wiped the remaining shaving cream off with a wet cloth and went right back to inspecting my pussy carefully. The hungry way he looked at my pussy was so tantalizing to watch.

"Yes," I moaned as he touched me.

"I love it when you shave me, Daddy," I said. My labia felt so bare and exposed, and every stroke of his fingers set my body on fire. I was slick with desire, even after the bath. I wondered if I would ever be not horny around him and hoped that I wouldn't. He moved his finger slowly, watching every twitch and moan with intense scrutiny.

"Do you want Daddy to make you cum

again?" his voice was so velvety smooth and sexy. His face was hovering just above my clit, and I could feel his hot breath wash over me. All he would have to do is reach out his tongue just a little.

"Yes, Daddy. Please lick my slutty pussy and let me cum all over your tongue," I moan. I was getting better at the dirty talk, but I probably would always blush just a little when I said such filthy things, as much as they made my pussy ache. Suddenly, he stopped. He pulled back and lifted me off the ground. I wrapped my legs around him eagerly, but he only put me back down onto my feet.

"No, that's enough for tonight, little one. It's bedtime now," I whimpered and pouted. My pussy felt like it was on fire. How could he do that to me, get me all hot and bothered and then leave me hanging?

"That was mean, Daddy!" I said, poking my lip out even further.

"You'd better wipe that pout off that cute

little face, baby girl. Daddy says no more, and that's how it's going to be," he ordered. He led me back into the bedroom.

"Do you want Daddy to put a diaper on you tonight or are you feeling like a big girl," he said. I was still upset, however. Being shaved by him had aroused me greatly, and I didn't like being denied release. I refused to answer him. Instead, I crossed my arms and pouted. His expression immediately grew stern.

"No, baby," he said firmly.

"What did I say about that pout. You have to learn that Daddy is in charge," he said. Again, I didn't answer him not verbally anyway. I scrunched up my face and stuck my tongue out at him. He sighed.

"Ok, baby girl, you asked for it," he said, shaking his head. He pulled my still-naked form over his knee and brought his hand down on my bottom. It hurt so much more than it had when I had my diaper on, even more than the playful smacks he had given me during our lovemaking. I jerked with every blow, tears springing to my eyes, and I try to wriggle my way off of his lap. I don't get far before he grabs my waist and pulls me back, spanking me even harder.

"Daddy, please! I'm sorry, I won't pout anymore," I cried.

"I know you're sorry," he said calmly, continuing to smack my bottom.

"But you have to learn your lesson. You have to learn that Daddy is in charge," he growled. I try to reach back to block the blows but quickly pinned my hands down with one hand while continuing to spank me with the other. I sobbed, and I kicked, but nothing I did made him stop. He didn't stop until my bottom was bright red, feeling like it was on fire. At last, he relented, rubbing my inflamed flesh lightly.

"Are you going to behave now?" he asked softly, his hand stroking my back and thighs as well.

"Yes, Daddy," I sniffled. He lay back on the bed, pulling me on top of him. My still damp hair fanned out around us as I nestled into his broad chest, wiping the tears from my eyes. The spanking had done nothing to quell my desire if anything the pain in my bottom only made me want him more, but I was determined to be a good girl for him.

"You took your spanking like a good girl, Daddy's proud of you," he whispered and rubbed my back. As he ran his hands over the tender flesh of my bottom, I winced.

"It hurts," I whined. Daddy chuckled and rolled me onto my back.

"It's supposed to hurt, sweetheart. That's what makes it a punishment. Now, every time you sit down over the next few days, you'll remember who you belong to," he said.

"I belong to you, Daddy," I said without hesitation, wrapping my arms sleepily around his neck.

"You sure do, baby girl," he murmured against my neck. I could tell that he was getting sleepy as well.

"You always will. I'm going to take care of you. I'll never let anything bad ever happen to you again," he said. We fell asleep like that, wrapped tightly in one another's arms.

Chapter 18

I awoke to feel something brush between my legs. I looked over to Daddy's pillow to see that he wasn't there. Then, I felt his tongue brush up against my clit. I moaned and opened my legs, eager to allow him more access.

"You're still wet from last night," he noted with satisfaction.

"You must need it bad," he added.

"Yes, Daddy. I do need it bad. I need YOU bad," I beg. I ran my fingers through his silky brown hair as he gave my pussy a long, slow lick, twirling his tongue around my swollen clit. He lapped at me, making my legs quiver. I threw my head back against the pillow and moaned.

"That's it, pumpkin," he said, sliding a finger into me.

"Show Daddy how much you like it. Play with your breasts," he said.

He resumed his attention to my clit but watched to make sure that I obeyed. I grabbed my breast and pinched my nipples as he watched in the dim predawn light. He slid his hands under my butt. My flesh was still bruised and sore, and it stung as he dug in his fingers, bringing my hips closer to his face. The combined sensations of pleasure and pain drew me closer to orgasm, and I squirmed against Daddy's mouth not sure if he would allow it. I whined and kicked my legs, trying to work up the courage to ask. Just then he stopped and repositioned himself on top of me. He kissed me deeply, his hot tongue sweeping into my mouth, making me ache for him. As we kissed, his hands circled my wrists, holding them down onto the mattress gently but firmly. It felt so good, his weight on top of me, holding me in place as his cock slowly worked its way into position.

"Would you like to cum on Daddy's cock, little one?" he asked sweetly, pressing himself against my entrance. I was thrilled. He had seemed to have read my mind.

"Yes, please. I love cumming on your cock, Daddy. It's my favorite," I said, smiling at him.

"I know it is darling. You can cum whenever you like, ok pumpkin?" He questioned.

"Oh, thank you. I need to cum so bad, Daddy," I gushed in relief. I crooned with happiness as he began to sink his cock into me, still holding me by the wrists. He entered me slowly, painfully slow actually. I tried to thrust my hips upwards to take more of him in, but his weight on top of me kept me pinned in place. I whimpered and pouted, but it was to no avail. The pleasure torture wasn't over yet, apparently. He maintained that excruciatingly slow pace until he was buried inside of me completely. He held himself there for a moment before pulling out again at that same incredibly slow speed.

"Daddy," I whined, trying to kick my legs under his heavy weight, trying to shift my hips, anything to stimulate myself.

"Please, I need to cum!" I begged.

"Go ahead, sweet girl," he said, his voice

heavy with fake innocence.

"Daddy already told you you could," he said.

"But I need - I need-," I stutter. He was sinking back into me, slowly splitting my pussy open, filling me up inch by inch.

"Please!" I beg.

"What is it that you need sweetheart? You can tell me. You can tell me anything," he said. I could tell he was trying not to smile.

"I need you to fuck me!" I cried out, hardly able to take any more. I needed relief, damn it!

"I am fucking you, sweetheart," he calmly replied. More feigned ignorance. *Cruel bastard.* I was on the verge of tears. His slow pumping felt so good but I just couldn't -

"Please, Daddy," I said, thrashing my head back and forth on the pillow. I was beyond all pride and all embarrassment. I was just pure, throbbing need.

"I need more. Please fuck me hard. I need you to pound me with your cock. Give it to me! Give me your cock, please!" I screamed. He laughed and let go of my wrists at last. I immediately began clawing at his back. I was desperate for release. I would do anything, say anything.

"Anything you say, sweetheart," he said with a sadistic grin and unleashed himself onto me. With wild, animalistic thrusts, he finally gave me the fucking that I needed, that I had begged him for. He spread my legs wide, pounding into me hard and fast. Every thrust made me go blind with pleasure. My whole world was centered on his cock, on the sweet, sweet fucking that he was giving me. I did not last long. I came undone beneath him, trembling as the peak took me over. I grabbed his hips and held on as he growled and pumped as I clenched around him. He pressed his forehead against mine as I relaxed against the sheets once more but did not let up his pace.

"Oh, yes, baby girl. That's so good," he moaned. His breath grew faster, panting, and growling in her ear. I was still feeling waves of pleasure from orgasm, and with every wild thrust,

I could feel myself building towards another. I loved knowing that I was causing so much pleasure in him, knowing that I was making him lose control. His hands grabbed at my breast, squeezing and playing with my nipples just as I had done earlier. We were both covered in sweat, and I could feel his muscles begin to tense, knew that he was getting closer to his climax as well. I could feel my pleasure rise to meet his.

"Oh, fuck, baby. You're so tight, so sexy. You make me so crazy. I'm so close. I love fucking you. I love you," he groaned. His words made me tighten around him, and he drove himself deep inside of me with one last thrust, flooding my pussy with his hot cum. I exploded around him, waves of pure joy and ecstasy overtook me. We shouted as we came together and fell back in a panting, sweaty heap. As I started to get my breath back, it slowly dawned on me what he had said at the very end.

"You love me?" I asked in the darkness. I wished I could see his face better at that moment, but it was still so early that it was dark out and all I could see was his silhouette. He sighed.

"Yes," he admittedly softly.

"I do love you. I've never been as happy as I've been since you came into my life. You're all I've been able to think about. I never knew what it would be like to have someone to come home to, someone to protect and look after. You make me so happy, Molly. You don't have to say it back if it's too early -" He said.

"I love you too," I interrupted, stopping that silly train of thought before it could even leave the station.

"Of course, I love you. You took me in when no one else would have me. You took care of me and made sure that I was happy and healthy. You're sexy and sweet and damn good in bed. How could I help but fall in love with you?" I said.

"Oh, baby girl," he whispered and pulled me close. He kissed me softly on my lips and squeezed me.

"You're more than I ever could have dreamed of. I promise to always be there for you," he said. He held me and kissed me until his alarm clock went off and only then did he reluctantly got out of bed. I studied his well-muscled form as he got dressed, his brown hair shining gold in the early morning light. His toned legs slid into his boxer briefs, and I could still see the swell of his manhood. The sight of him stirred my heart just as much as it did my body.

How did I get so incredibly lucky? I can't believe that he's mine. All mine, I thought, not for the first time and certainly not for the last.

"What would you like for breakfast, baby girl?" he asked, reaching for his pants.

Chapter 19

I never did find an apartment or even look for one, for that matter. A year later, Bill and I are still happily living together. We have settled into a nice routine. Every morning, he updates my itinerary so that I always know where I have to be and when. Then, he makes us breakfast, and we eat in silence. I like it quiet in the mornings. Bill likes it when I give him a blowjob under the table before he leaves for work every morning. He says it is the best part of waking up. If I am home when he returns from work in the evening, he has me meet him by the front door, naked and ready to blow him again. Most nights, the blowing turns to fucking. Sometimes, I am out at a class or my therapy appointment, and he beats me home. On those nights, I get even more vigorous fucking as soon as I walk in the door. Even after a year together, he still can't keep his hands off of me. As he fucks me, he tells me how much he has missed me and how he couldn't stop thinking about me the whole time we were apart. Often, my itinerary includes taking sexy pics, either in lingerie, he had bought for me or completely naked, and then texting them to him throughout the day. On those days, we fuck all night long.

I still wear my diaper, but not all the time. How little I feel varies from day to day. Both Bill and Dr. Saperstein say that is normal. I still haven't met any other littles, but I would like to. Bill says there are all kinds of littles out there of different genders, ages, and sizes. I'd like to have them all over for a play date someday. I've made a few friends online but no one close by yet. Bill says we will keep looking. I have made other friends, of course. I don't share this particular part of my life with them.

Sometimes, when I am in my little space, I will sleep in my room at night. Having my own space no longer makes me nervous. The first night that I spent in my bed, Daddy gallantly offered to sleep on the floor so that he could catch any monsters that might have been hanging around, looking for little girls to munch on. Knowing that he was nearby and that I was safe made it easy for me to drift off and it hasn't been a problem since. Most nights, however, I sleep in Daddy's bed. He is always coming up with fun, sexy games for us to try and fun, sexy toys for us to play with. I don't always like the games or toys, and he never forces them on me. He is happy to toss them out no matter how much money or time he had spent on them.

"If you're not interested, then neither am I," he would always say and that would be that.

Tonight, we played my favorite game of all. Bill's face wrinkled in concentration. He held his breath, his whole body tense, before letting it out in a triumphant cry.

"Triple word score! Beat that," he yelled and gleefully counted up his points from the Scrabble tiles and added them to the score sheet. I groaned, looking at the numbers in despair. I was whooped.

"Come on, it's your turn," he said, nudging me.

"I don't want to play anymore," I pout.

"What a sore loser!" He exclaimed. I can tell how much he was enjoying this rare opportunity to gloat. I usually had the high score on Scrabble night.

"It's a tactful retreat," I said, trying to sound serious. He starts to tickle me.

"Turn that frown upside down baby girl," he said, making me laugh. Despite my grumpiness over his victory, I giggled. Seeing a crack in my pouting facade, he leaned in for a kiss. As his warm lips covered mine, I immediately forget all about the game. I grabbed onto him like a baby koala, my legs wrapping around his waist and my arms wrapping around his neck. He moans into my mouth, and I can feel him get instantly hard. As our tongues meet, a burning heat stirs inside of me. I am hungry for him. He grabs my ass, leaning me back on the couch and pulling me closer against him. I spread my legs wider, knocking over the board. Tiles are scattered everywhere, but we hardly notice as we tear at each other's clothing. He pulls my shirt off and captures my nipple with his teeth. Knowing just how much pressure to apply, which is a lot, he teases me, watching me writhe beneath him. He squeezes my breasts together and buries his face there, licking and nibbling. I ache to feel his skin on mine and pull at his shirt, whining with impatience as it gets tangled up in his arms.

"Hold on, baby girl," he said, pulling it off for me, "so impatient." He settles back on top of me, and I run my hands over the muscles of his back, over the light sprinkling of hair on his chest, lightly grazing his nipples. Our naked flesh presses together as he kisses me again. He pulls me against him tightly, wrapping me up in his warm, strong arms. I know that I am exactly where I belong. I have finally found my home, and it is here in his arms. He lifts my skirt and takes in a sharp breath of air when he sees that I'm not wearing any panties. I like to surprise him with that every once in a while, and it always gets a reaction. He looks at me like the big bad wolf about to gobble up little red, and the analogy makes me giggle.

"Oh, you're in trouble now, little one," he said with a grin and lowered himself. He takes me in with a deep breath, savoring the scent of me. He teases me lightly with his tongue, grazing my labia and clit casually, not wanting to overwhelm me with too much pleasure at once.

"Hold your legs open for Daddy," he said. I obey, always more than happy to be ordered around by him. His dominance in the bedroom remains one of my favorite things about him. I grip my thighs, holding my legs akimbo as he continues to explore my dripping slit with his tongue. He moans as he tastes me, bathing me with long slow licks. I watch him, hypnotized and he works his way inward, seeking out my clit. I moan when he finds it, almost forgetting to do as he instructed and running my hands through his soft locks instead. Almost. I'm much better trained these days, and I know that will earn me a time-out at the very least.

My hands stay in place as he twirls his tongue around my button. I whimper, my legs quivering as he laps at me faster. He sinks a finger into my tight, hole, looking up at me with an evil glimmer in his eye, knowing that I'm already close to a climax. Only I can't because he hasn't permitted me yet. I know from the look in his eyes that it will be a long evening and that permission is still a long way away. Slowly, he slides in a second finger, stretching me out in the most delicious way. I lose track of everything else in the world; all I am aware of are his fingers pumping in and out of me as his tongue traces circles of ecstasy over my clit. All I can do is hold my legs open and try not to cum like a good girl. Finally, he stops torturing my pussy with pleasure. Standing over me, he pulls his pants and boxers down, freeing his rock hard penis. I can't take my eyes off of it or him as he slowly licks the fingers that have just been inside of me and then wraps them around the head of his cock. He strokes it as he gazes into my eyes, watching my expression get hungrier by the minute. He loves teasing me, making me wait for it, making me beg for it even. He loves to hear me beg.

"Turn over," he said. I shift my weight and roll over onto my tummy.

"Ass in the air," he said. I love this position. His voice is gruff and commanding, making my body thrill with arousal. I am his to command, and he knows it. Again, he makes me wait, ass up, as he pleasures himself. My pussy is throbbing, but I wait, knowing full well that it will be well worth it. He smacks my ass, lightly. This is a sexy spanking, not a punishment spanking. I smile as he spanks me again, just hard enough to sting. Just hard enough to make my pussy tingle. I moan and hold my ass up higher, eager for more spankings. They rain down until my entire ass is on fire and my pussy is dripping onto the couch. I wait, panting in the silence. He grabs me by the hair and brings my mouth to his cock. I lick him eagerly

"That's it, baby," he moaned.

"Suck me down. Take me deep. Daddy's filthy girl," he said as I moan around his cock. I love the dirty names he calls me. I love being dirty for him and him alone. He plunges in cock in deep, making me choke and drool, knowing just how much I can take and just how much will leave me aching for more. He knows that with every thrust down my throat, the fire in my pussy only grows hotter. I make sure to keep my ass in the air, aware that he has not instructed otherwise and that is likely enjoying the view as he slowly fucks my throat.

He sits on the couch and pulls me onto his lap. He pulls my skirt up over my head, leaving me naked. I straddle his lap, and he starts licking and nibbling my breasts again. He positions his cock near my entrance but doesn't plunge in just yet.

"Play with yourself," he muttered around a mouthful of my nipple.

"Let's see how horny baby girl can get," he said, smiling. I rub my clit, driven wild by his mouth on me and by his cock, so tantalizingly close. I know I shouldn't rub too hard, he still hasn't given me permission to cum, but he feels so damn good. He grabs my ass, pulling my cheeks apart, giving them the occasional slap. I know that can tell that I am getting dangerously close.

"Watch it little one. Who do you belong to?" He asked. I whimper softly, but I slow down.

"I belong to you, Daddy," I reply, knowing where this is going.

"And who does this pussy belong to?" He pushes his cock against me, nudging toward my slick entrance. I gasp and moan, trying to find the words he wants to hear.

"This pussy belongs to you," I manage to say between clenched teeth. He sinks into me a little bit deeper, stretching me. His fingers dig into the flesh of my buttocks, tightly controlling the pace, delighting in the way my eyes roll back into my head as he impales me with his cock.

"Good girl," he whispers.

"Nice and slow. That's a good little slut," he

said, slapping my ass and groping it with both hands. My back arches as he finally fully inside of me, still playing with my clit.

"Ride me, baby girl," he said, leaning back to enjoy the show. He knows that letting me set the pace is dangerous, that I am liable to forget myself and let myself go before I'm allowed to. I will have to be extra careful. I move my hips slowly, sliding up and down the length of him as I stare into his eyes. I edge myself on his cock, pausing when I need to, gritting my teeth as I use every ounce of my willpower to keep myself from losing control.

"Mmm, my baby girl needs it badly, doesn't she?" He questions.

"Yes, Daddy! I need to cum so bad. Please, please, please ..." I trailed off, so enraptured by lust that I forget to beg. He laughs and twists my nipples lightly, making me gasp.

"Oh, I know you can do better than that. Beg like a good girl and Daddy will let you cum," he said. I whimper and slow down my pace, trying to focus. His cock was so distracting.

"Please, Daddy. I want to cum on your cock so bad. I've been a good girl. Please let me cum. Your cock feels so good, so hard inside my slutty little pussy. Please, Daddy, can I?" I beg.

"Much better," he growls. He grips me by the hips and flips me onto my back, spreading my legs wide as he plunges into me, hard and deep.

"You can cum now, baby girl," he orders. He slams into me, fast and furious. I wrap my thighs around him and hold on as my orgasm erupts. My head snaps back, and I moan with abandon. He has turned me into quite the screamer.

"That's right, sweetie, cum for Daddy," he said. He kisses my sweaty neck, and I tremble underneath him. Shivers of pleasure run through me even after the main wave breaks. His thrusts do not slow down, he keeps pounding into me, wrapped up in his own pleasure now.

"Oh, darling. You get so wet when you cum — such a sweet, dirty girl. You make Daddy feel so good," he said. I love how vocal he gets when he fucks me. I never get tired of being reassured that I am his fantasy, his perfect girl. His hands clench and unclench, and I know that he is close.

"Fuck yeah, baby girl. Keep taking it just like that. Oh, you're such a good girl. Daddy's good little slut. Here it comes!" He moans. He goes completely still, except for his cock which is pumping away inside of me, filling me with hot cum. With a groan, he goes limp against me, burying his head into my breast. He holds me close to him, still inside me, until he regains his breath. A feeling of complete contentment washes over me. I know that in a moment, we will have to clean up the substantial mess we've made but for now, I hold his sweaty brow to my chest and thank my lucky stars that he came into my life.

Chapter 20

That evening, as he is giving me my bath, he starts asking me about vacation spots. At first, it seems like another fun game, fantasizing about all the exotic places we would like to travel to someday. As the discussion gets more and more specific, with details about vacation time and airfare, I realize that it's more than that.

"Wait, are you serious?" I ask. I have never been on a trip before, and the idea is exciting.

"Well, maybe not right away. I was just sort of thinking, you know ..." He trailed off and blushed. I hadn't seen him blush since he asked me to move in with him.

"You were thinking ..." I prompted. What on earth could have him so nervous?

"I was thinking, well I was wondering, actually, where you might want to go when we went on our honeymoon ... someday ... maybe..." He blushed, even more, deeper than I had ever seen before.

"Did you - did you just propose to me?" I questioned. A surge of adrenaline swept over my body.

"No!" he sputtered.

"I wouldn't propose to you in a bathroom. I would do it nicer than that. You know, romantic. Rinse," he said. I leaned my head back as he rinsed the suds from my hair. Silently, I think about what he said as he helps me out of the bathtub and dries my hair. He towels me off and helps me into my pajamas, tonight I've chosen a diaper and a onesie. He combs my hair and splits my hair into pigtails, fastening them with small rubber bands. He carries me to bed and finds Hamilton, putting him on the pillow beside me.

"Tahiti," I say, finally reaching a decision.

"What?" he asks, seemingly forgotten the topic at hand.

"For our honeymoon. I think I would like to go to Tahiti. I hear it's beautiful. What do you think?" I ask, smiling. He grinned, leaning down to kiss my forehead.

"I think I'd better start planning a trip to Tahiti," he said winking at me.

Connor's Little One

A Romantic Novel About a Daddy Dom who Trains His Baby Girl in the DDLG and ABDL Kink

By Tina Moore

Chapter 1

The drive to the office was always mundane. What else could be expected with morning traffic? I could have avoided it altogether if I left earlier, but I didn't do that for two reasons. The first was that there was no way in hell I wanted to go to the office at all, much less earlier than was necessary. The second—related to the first in that I'd have to wake up earlier than usual—was that the term *morning person* didn't suit me in the slightest. Still, I suppose there were worse things as I pulled into the parking lot. I parked above ground because no one else did. It made the rush to leave a lot faster, albeit hotter when everyone who'd parked underground had to wait in a long line of cars as if they were getting some kind of head start on rush hour. Nevertheless, just because things could be worse didn't mean I had to enjoy them as they were. And I so didn't.

I probably wouldn't have hated the drive to work

if I didn't hate my job so much, but the truth is that I hated my job. My position in life was boring, repetitive, and going nowhere slowly. The woman who raised me would have said I was a stubborn little brat, ungrateful for that which others would love to have, and perhaps she would be right. Perhaps I was ungrateful. Perhaps I should have been happier with my job. Perhaps things weren't so bad.

Only, as I walked into the office, I didn't care whether she was right or not. It was pretty bad as far as I was concerned. A musty smell, reminiscent of Grandma's old cupboards filled with mothballs, hit my nose and I knew I'd have to suffer through it all day. I spritzed a bit of my sweet-smelling perfume in the hopes that my own scent might distract me, knowing that I'd have to do it a dozen more times over the course of the day. The place buzzed and hummed with the sound of technology, computers and copiers and outdated fax machines all hard at work. Possibly the worst thing about the office was the color of the walls; a horrible sickly green that reminded me all-too-much of a doctor's office.

I didn't work in a doctor's office. I was not greeted with a waiting room full of sick, coughing patients. Still, a part of me wondered if it would have been a better environment.

No, my boss was not a doctor curing a world full of disease. Sure, he helped people, but the question was to what end?

At that moment, my boss materialized, walking through to his office—the one with a view and a door—in freshly polished shoes and a crisp navy suit. He didn't look at me as he passed by, but then he never did. Lawyers didn't look at their secretaries in this office unless absolutely necessary. Yes, secretary was my working title, complete with a small cubicle and a computer slower than the morning traffic. The man I worked for was a ruthless district attorney who defended, well, bad men.

"Slumming, I see," a voice suddenly spoke over the top of the cubicle.

"Excuse me?" I looked up to find an incredibly pretty blonde woman staring at me, the corner of her perfect crimson lips curled into a smirk.

I didn't have to see the other side of the cubicle to know that Lisa was probably wearing a short dress that hugged her figure and matched her lipstick, worlds apart from me in my pantsuit. I knew the way to the top. The only problem was that I didn't want to reach it that way, especially not if my competition was Lisa.

"Oh, nothing," she waved her hand dismissively.

"You look tired today. Were you out last night?" She looked at me with her evil-looking eyes already knowing the answer.

"No," I answered blandly. Lisa knew I wasn't out last night. Lisa asked questions such as this one to goad me. Lisa would deny it, but she loved getting underneath my skin.

"I thought I saw you at the party, but I guess not. Now that I think of it, that woman was wearing a really cute dress." Her pretty blue eyes roved up and down my body, taking in my pantsuit and old black pumps in a way that made my stomach turn.

"So, it couldn't have been you," she quickly added before flicking her hair. Before I could respond, Lisa turned and walked away, her hair swinging as she went. The light glinted off it, and I secretly reveled in the fact that it wasn't her natural color. Unfortunately for me, Lisa was too vain ever to let her roots start to show.

Needless to say, the start of my day was not a good one. For the rest of the day, I went through my duties while staring at the clock, wishing that time might go by a tiny bit faster. I had to resist the urge to slam things—my keys on the keyboard, my phone on its receiver, my fist through the computer screen. The only saving grace was that I was alone. My boss, Mr. Jones, didn't bother me. As much as I hated it, I did my job well, well enough that no one felt the need to check on me throughout the day. I might have been more inclined to leave my job as a secretary sooner if that were the case.

As it was, the day passed by slowly, and it was filled with the thought that I was bored and wasted in a law firm. By the time the clock finally ticked over to six p.m., I needed a drink. I was keenly aware of the fact that I was one of the first people out of the office and, due to my clever parking job in the baking hot sun, one of the first out of the parking lot too.

***

"Well, well, well," Connor murmured at the sight of me. He was drying a glass behind the bar, a glass I knew was just for me.

"It's been a while since I saw the likes of you here," he said, throwing the bar towel over his shoulder.

"The likes of me?" I raised my eyebrows, taking my seat in a barstool across from him, but it was hard not to smile.

"You've been a stranger lately, little miss," Connor said as he sat my drink down in front of me. It was my usual, a milkshake cocktail with more strawberries than alcohol, made just the way I liked it. The dimple in Connor's cheek appeared as I took a sip, reminding me for the thousandth time that my *baby girl* drink, as he called it, amused him to no end.

"Shut up," I mumbled shyly, color rushing to my cheeks.

"A woman can want both alcohol and a milkshake at the end of the day, you know," I said trying to assert my grown up authority. This only made Connor grin more.

"Oh, I never said that a woman couldn't," he mused, pursing his lips together to stop his smirk. Something about the way he said *woman* made me squirm in my seat as if I didn't quite qualify. Then again, I supposed it was difficult for anyone to look like an adult standing next to Connor, much less sitting across from him. The man was a giant, from his towering height all the way down to his tree-trunk thighs. He was built like a brick wall, and I was pretty sure he didn't even know how intimidating his appearance could be. Of course, then he would smile, and those dimples would come out, making butterflies swirl in the stomach of every woman within a five-mile radius.

"So? Aren't you going to tell me about all your woes?" Connor raised his eyebrows.

"What makes you think I have woes?" I questioned amused at his choice of words.

"Why else would you be here on a Monday night?" He replied, clearly impressed with himself.

Dammit. How much more obvious could I get? I looked around. The bar was quieter than usual, but that was to be expected for a Monday. I heaved a sigh and looked back to find that Connor was staring at me. If his expression could speak, it would be saying, "Uh-huh. That's what I thought."

"Okay, okay," I rolled my eyes before adding, "I have the Monday Blues."

"Don't roll your eyes at me," he murmured warningly.

"Now, get talking, little one," Connor said leaning against the bar. I was used to this sort of behavior. Connor had been bossy from the day I met him. It was just the way he was. That didn't make me feel any less like I'd been reprimanded though, and so, I sipped my milkshake cocktail until there was nothing left.

"I'm listening," Connor stated. In his hand, he held another milkshake cocktail, which held my attention far more than he did.

"Don't even think about it. No talking, no milkshake," he teased, matching my exasperated expression.

"Fine. I had a shitty day at work. But there's nothing new there. I always hate work," I snapped.

And you for damn sure already know that, I thought to myself. I didn't miss the way he flinched when I swore. This time, however, he knew better than to call me out for my language. I wasn't sure what it was, but Connor hated it when I cursed or cussed. Truth be told, I went to the bar more often than I cared to admit, but could anyone blame me? There were alcoholic milkshakes, for goodness' sake! The music wasn't bad either, but nothing topped Connor and his sage advice. Don't even get me started on his heavy pouring hand. In truth, the bartender had become one of my best friends over the past few months. He was always willing to listen to me.

"Wanna talk about it?" He asked, softening, which only made me roll my eyes.

"There's nothing to talk about, really. I guess I'm just tired of going through the same old thing every day, you know? Life is so boring. I wish there were some kind of escape from it all," I replied, placing my head in my hands.

"And what if there was?" Connor almost interrogated. I looked at him and squinted my eyes.

"Was what?" I questioned, unsure of what his mysterious tone was hiding.

"An escape, little one. What if I told you that you could easily get away from it all and the only thing you needed was your imagination?" He asked simply. He slid my glass to me, and I started sipping, creating a pink, frothy, milkshake mustache on my upper lip.

"Sign me up," I laughed, happy to be getting my milkshake, dancing contently in my seat. Connor chuckled and grabbed a napkin, reaching across the bar to wipe the ice cream off of my lip. My breath caught in my throat at the close proximity. It wasn't fair that he was that much bigger than me. He barely had to lean forward over the bar to reach. It was difficult to concentrate on anything when he was that close and, truth be told, I sucked at holding my liquor. My head was as fuzzy as my tummy, and all I could think was that Connor was really warm. If I were anyone else, if I lived in any other life, I would have asked Connor out. But of course, I wouldn't. I was me, plain old Jessie, and there was no way a man like Connor would ever go for me. It's for that reason that I blame alcohol for what I said next.

"Are you just looking for an excuse to get close to me?" I teased, surprised at myself. Connor arched a brow, and I found myself staring into his striking blue eyes, holding my breath as I waited for the response.

"Do I need an excuse?" He asked, leaning back and showing off his big biceps.

Oh, my God. What am I doing? This is Connor! My mind was yelling at me as my eyes glazed over. The more I thought about it though, the more I thought this is Connor. He was tall, extremely good looking and always had the attention of some girl at the bar. Perhaps it was the fact that I knew him that made him so damn appealing, the way he was always there for me, and indeed even the way he was cleaning my froth mustache off at that very moment, though it made me feel small.

"You know," he finally continued, as if I weren't embarrassingly silent regarding his question. He continued to wipe my lip gently.

"I think I know just what you need," he said as he looked at me with an intense stare.

"Oh, yeah?" I asked with all the cheek I could muster while having a grown man wipe away milkshake froth from my face.

"And what's that?" I quickly added, trying not to slur my words.

"Well, for one thing, someone to put you in your place when you get cheeky," Connor said to my sheer surprise. I raised my eyebrows as he finally pulled back.

"Is that so?" I teased, not wanting to give up all my control over this conversation. Connor merely nodded matter-of-factly.

"You need a Daddy, Jessie," he said, making my head freeze as I heard him say my name. I made the terrible mistake of taking another sip of my drink and at his words, began coughing as it went down the wrong pipe. I could barely breathe as I spluttered, and before I knew it, Connor had hopped over the bar. His warm hand was on my back, gently patting, and was he cooing to me? It was getting too uncomfortable. I willed myself to breathe normally again and, with red and watery eyes, finally stopped coughing in time to catch my breath. I looked up at Connor, who seemed even larger on this side of the bar.

"What on earth are you talking about?" I said, shaking my head trying to focus on his words.

"I'm talking about a Daddy or a Daddy Dom more specifically," he began to explain. He tilted his head, and I could tell he was amused by my confusion. Apparently, I was funny. Who knew?

"And what exactly is a *Daddy Dom*?" I asked with probably more attitude than I should, considering the way he'd talked about putting me in my place. The thought alone made me shrink. I couldn't help but look Connor up and down. This was the first time there wasn't a bar between us, and well, it was kind of hard not to look.

"See, even if you don't know it, you still crave it," he said in a low voice.

"You want a Daddy who will tell you what to do, discipline you when you give too much attitude, and take you like you've never been taken before," he explained, sending a shiver down my spine. I didn't respond. I didn't know how to. All I knew was, for some reason, something deep within my center heated at his words. No, it wasn't his words. It was the way he said them. Close to me, close enough that I could feel his hot breath against the skin of my neck, and in an almost animalistic growl.

"You see, Jessie, I think you're a little girl deep down inside," Connor plainly said as he began to serve another customer.

Chapter 2

The morning brought with it several things. The sunshine filtering through my bedroom window, and the sound of birdsong woke me. Normally, these would have been welcomed, though when I felt the familiar throbbing of my head, I wished the silence of the night hadn't left. I'd have gladly rejected the sunlight too, my retinas complaining about the pain. At least I hadn't been woken by my alarm clock. My head might have exploded if that were the case. Thankfully, I was off work for the day. I wasn't so sure I would have had quite that many milkshakes the previous evening if I weren't.

How many had I had? I thought to myself. As my feet touched the floor, and I made my way toward the bathroom, everything came back to me. The memories were a blur at first, but by the time I'd climbed out of the shower, everything became startlingly clear, and I didn't know how to feel about it all. By the time I'd left the bar, I'd had three milkshakes, a couple of shots, and entirely too much Connor the Hot Bartender. Make that Connor the Daddy Dom as I now knew him.

The only problem was that I didn't know what a Daddy Dom was exactly. I mean, he tried to explain it to me, but by then, I was on my third milkshake and rather enjoying how close he was standing to me. It didn't hurt that he smelled really nice. I shut my eyes and groaned as more memories came back.

"And let me guess, you think you could be my Daddy? Put a Little Girl like me in my place?" I asked as I watched him shoot his whiskey.

"Oh, I don't think it. I know it." He had added as he watched me leave. I couldn't believe I'd asked such a thing. I'd always been a little flirty when I had too much to drink, and goodness knew I had a bad attitude. The few ex-boyfriends I'd had over the years called me a brat more times than I cared to count. Throw in a seriously attractive guy who seemed happy enough to flirt back, and I had a recipe for disaster. How was I ever going to go back to the bar again?

Still, regardless of my tipsy humiliation, Connor's words stuck with me, and I wondered what he meant by them. He didn't elaborate further, mostly because I hadn't asked, but in spite of myself, I was unbelievably curious. That's why the second I was dressed, I found myself sitting behind my computer with an incognito tab open. Little did I know it would be the first of many open tabs.

"What are you doing, Jessie?" I asked myself, heaving a sigh as I hit enter on the search bar. A thousand links regarding *DDLG* and *ABDL* showed up, and I quickly realized that the world was full of people practicing this particular kink. I would have expected a minority to be interested, but the overwhelming amount of information proved there were a lot more people into it than I'd initially imagined. And so, with no small amount of confusion, I began my learning journey. It was easy enough to find all the sexual stuff about the kinks, but what I didn't expect was the fact that it was clearly stated on every site that the relationship could be completely devoid of sex. I discovered that, as Connor had already told me, DDLG stood for Daddy Dom and Little Girl whereas ABDL stood for Adult Baby and Diaper Lover. They seemed totally bizarre at first, but the more I read, the more I found that they were incredibly loving relationships.

I was able to find some forums in which Daddy Doms and Little Girls actually communicated! Reading through them, I was astonished by the care plainly evident in the messages and questions. They were kind of cute, the longer I lingered. The Daddy Doms were caring and kind, taking care of their Littles as if they were legitimate children, and the Littles were carefree and happy.

The more I read, the more I wished I was as happy as they were. I searched why Littles were so happy, and that's when I found out about *Little Space*, a wonderful mindset that Littles went into at will. In this mindset, they thought and acted a younger age than they actually were. As far as I could tell, this varied from person to person and depended on their "age." Littles actually chose to act a specific age, any age they wanted, even two years old if that's what brought them joy. And they did the things that a person of that age did. This could be anything from coloring to wearing diapers.

One thing was clear to me though; Littles generally used Little Space to escape from the stress and troubles of their day-to-day lives. Simply put, they were people who enjoyed pretending to be younger than they actually were as a way to relieve themselves from their responsibilities. They shrugged their adult-self off in exchange for some carefree time doing something that made them happy, even if that was drinking from a baby bottle.

Biting down on my lower lip, I decided that was quite enough reading up on the kinks. My cheeks were hot, and I was consumed by an unexpected burning desire. To my shock, I really wanted to try Little Space out. A small part of me didn't want

Connor to be right, though after reading up on Littles, I was starting to believe that I simply wanted to rebel against him. Supposedly, Littles were supposed to be bratty. I didn't really like the idea of being nothing more than a stereotype. It made me pouty. A larger part, however, didn't care and kind of liked the idea of standing up to Connor, as if I was a brat.

I shook that thought off immediately. This was Connor. Yes, he was super attractive and sweet Connor, but he was also really bossy and intimidating Connor. And I didn't quite know how to feel about the heat that I felt in the pit of my belly at the idea of what Connor might do if I decided to stand up to him, especially after everything I'd read.

When did I start thinking about Connor as if he were a tasty morsel? I thought, a sudden rush of excitement flooding m veins.

I wasn't sure. Perhaps I'd always had some kind of hidden attraction for him. This realization only got me thinking about how Connor saw me. Was he attracted to me? If his flirting and that dominant way he'd breathed into my ear were anything to go by, that was a resounding yes. Had he always felt this way? I didn't know. The idea of someone like Connor looking at me as if I were a tasty morsel didn't seem possible.

Pushing thoughts of Connor and Daddy Doms away, I went back to thoughts of Little Space. After all, what could it hurt? I wasn't sure Connor was right about me needing a Daddy, but I definitely needed some kind of escape from my reality and from my horrible job in particular. Truthfully, I wasn't turned off by the idea of coloring books and, to my surprise, baby bottles. In fact, there was a lot that I wasn't turned off by in terms of the DDLG and ABDL lifestyle.

Once the computer was off, I made my way to my closet in search of something Little to wear. If I was going to try it out, this seemed as good a place as any. Absently, I wondered how things had changed so quickly. Only the day before, I was a normal person who drank too much when life got tough and hated my job. Now, I was trying on a bright pink dress dotted with yellow flowers in the hopes it might make me feel free.

The dress was tighter than it had been once upon a time, but as I twirled in the mirror, I had to admit that I looked and felt really cute. I giggled at my reflection, giving another twirl, this time stretching my arms out on either side of me.

The dress was sweet and innocent, frilly around the hem and modest around the neckline. It had been for a baby shower I once attended—the guests were all meant to dress in the adult version of something a baby girl would wear since the mother, a colleague named Caroline, was expecting a girl. At least I'd bothered to follow the dress code. Some of the guests had done the bare minimum, wearing their hair a certain way or bedazzling their dresses, if they'd made any effort at all. Looking back on it, I was the only one who'd put in a great deal of effort, going so far as to tie my hair into pigtails complete with pink ribbons. I didn't care that I got strange stares from the other guests. Caroline loved my outfit.

Pink ribbons. I'm sure I still have those around here somewhere, I thought running to my bathroom cupboard.

***

It was a Friday night, and that meant the music from the bar was loud enough that I could feel the bass vibrating through my tiny car where I was parked outside. Coming back here took a lot of courage, so much so that I didn't think I had any left to get out of the car. Yet I knew I was going to have to see him again sooner or later, not that I thought he would make some kind of arrangement to see me or that I would run into him at the grocery store. Such things had never happened before. I didn't expect them to start now.

However, I would be lying if I said that I didn't *want* to see Connor again. The fact of the matter was that I really wanted to see him again, probably more than might be considered healthy. It had been exactly one month since I'd been to the bar and discovered the truth about DDLG and ABDL, exactly one month since he'd told me that I needed a Daddy.

Since that day, I discovered a lot about myself. One of the things I discovered was that he was right. I needed a Daddy. After weeks of testing myself and exploring my Little Space, an act that involved no small amount of shopping I might add, I was certain that I was a Little Girl. He'd been right all along, and that begged the question: what else was he right about?

"Dammit," I sighed, slamming the palm of my hand down on the top of the steering wheel. That turned out to be a terrible mistake as I cried out in pain.

"Dammit!" I repeated as my hand now throbbed. Finally, I climbed out of the car and made my way inside. It was busier than the last time I'd been there but not nearly as busy as the nightclubs in the surrounding areas. That was one of the things I liked about the place. Based on the pounding bass, one would expect it to be packed. Instead, it was filled with loyal regulars, and the music wasn't the usual electro stuff that could cause seizures even without all the flashing strobe lights. Classics played from a renovated jukebox in the back, hooked up to a massive sound system.

I spotted him the moment I walked in. He was talking to a leggy brunette in a skintight dress, and I felt the slightest twinge of jealousy. However, that faded away the moment he looked up at me. His hair complimented his eyes in the most flattering way, and his dimples came out as he smiled at me. It wasn't the cheeky smirk I was used to. This was a full-blown smile, showing off his pearly whites and touching his piercing eyes.

God, that smile was enough to make any woman's knees go weak, let alone a Little Girl's, I thought with a gulp. I stood up straight and walked over to the bar, resisting the urge to grin when the brunette looked me up and down. It was quite apparent that she noticed Connor's shift in attention. Against my better judgment, a surge of triumph shot through me, giving me the boost of confidence that I didn't know I needed.

Chapter 3

Any other day, I would have sat in a different seat. I would have waited for Connor to come to me for the sole purpose of pumping me with alcohol. I would have left the seat directly across from him, the one right beside the leggy brunette, empty.

There was something about the way Connor looked at me that night, though. I was filled with a certainty that his smile was meant for me and me alone, each of my steps leading me right toward it. When I took my place across from him, the brunette seemed to think as much as well because she got up with an indignant sound and walked away, after shooting both Connor and I a dirty look.

"I don't think she was a very happy customer," I pointed out.

"I'm afraid I accept tips based on the drinks, not the services… I might offer after hours," he stated, arching a brow.

"And I can tell you right now which one she was more interested in," he added. I bit down on my lower lip, unsure of how to respond. I wasn't sure what to say at all. Things had gone differently in my mind. I thought I could saunter up to the bar, though I'd never sauntered before in my life, and Connor would simply become putty in my hands. That clearly wasn't going to happen, and my hands were sweaty with nervousness.

"Can I get you a cocktail?" He offered.

"Yes, please." I didn't bother correcting him. We both knew they were milkshakes. Connor grabbed a glass and began preparing the drink.

"You look really nice tonight," he commented. "I especially like the hair."

"Yeah?" I asked. Warmth flooded my cheeks. I'd worn my hair in pigtails in the hopes Connor would like it, complete with pink ribbons. He nodded, watching me curiously as he slid my glass toward me and leaned over the bar.

"You know, I wasn't sure I'd ever see you again. I kind of thought I'd scared you away,"

Connor confessed. I sipped my milkshake. The taste alone reminded me of the last time I saw Connor and everything that transpired between us. This time, there was no denying that I was attracted to the man. It was amazing how much had changed in such a short time. Perhaps I'd always been attracted to him somewhere deep in my subconscious. The fact that he was a different person to me now seemed as if it should have changed things. This was the guy who'd told me about DDLG and ABDL. Never in my wildest dreams did I imagine I might be sitting in front of him, pondering what it might be like practicing the kinks with him.

"I'm glad you came back," Connor broke into my thoughts, his voice barely louder than a whisper. It was the breathiness in his words that caused goosebumps to rise on every inch of my skin.

"And I'm proud of you," he said, making my stomach tighten, and my bottom lip be bitten involuntarily.

"You're proud of me?" I said softly, feeling excited, and nauseous all in one go.

"You heard me right," he nodded before adding, "I'm proud of you for doing your homework."

"My, my homework?" Suddenly, I felt exposed, as if he could see right through me.

"You know exactly what I'm talking about, little one," the stern tone of his voice sent my belly into yet another somersault.

"You did your research. And I'm proud of you," he simply said once again. In spite of myself, I grinned up at him. I was so happy that I could have danced around like a little kid. I didn't do that, of course. I had to maintain some kind of air of dignity and decorum. My feet might have done a little jig where he couldn't see them though.

"So, what did you think of your findings?" He asked, tilting his head curiously. For some reason, the fact that we were in a bar didn't matter. There were people all around us, and anyone could have eavesdropped on the conversation, but I didn't care. Everything faded away, except for us. The sound of the music, the dim lights, and the scent of alcohol no longer existed. The only thing that really mattered was Connor and me speaking casually as we had a million times before, even if the subject matter wasn't what one would call casual.

And yet, I had no idea how to answer the question at hand.

"I... uhm... well..." I stammered. I took a deep breath to steady myself and tried again.

"The truth is I'm kind of interested in it," I confessed looking down into my glass. Connor reached across the bar, taking one of my pigtails between his fingertips and stroking it lightly.

"I kind of figured that part out for myself. What I really want to know is what brought you back here. To me," he boldly said clearly impressed with himself. When he stood back up, he crossed his arms over his chest, and I could hardly gather my thoughts. They were too busy obsessing over how muscular his body was. His biceps bulged beneath the form-fitting black shirt he wore and the shirt itself hinted at the lines of strength that lay beneath.

"I want to learn more," I blurted out, causing him to arch a brow, this time at me.

"I want to learn more about it. And well, I figured who better to teach me than you?" I said, taking the biggest gamble of my life. The dimples in Connor's cheeks made an appearance, but the corners of his mouth only twitched as if he wanted to smile.

"Dinner. Tomorrow night. Wear a diaper," he said almost in dot point form. I stared at him, trying to figure out how to respond to that, but I had no words.

"It wasn't a question. I'm taking you to dinner. If you want me to teach you, I'm happy to, but there will be a contract with rules." This time, he did smile, and I felt almost as if I were prey to a predator.

"Do you agree to this, little one?" Connor asked.

"I..." Taking a deep breath, I said the words I knew he wanted to hear, though I never expected them to make me press my thighs together the way I did.

"Yes, Daddy," I said breathlessly.

***

The first thing I discovered about adult diapers is that none of them were particularly flattering. The baby diapers were cute. They came in different colors, and some of them had images of teddy bears and candy and more all over them. If there was any chance they would have fit me, I'd have gotten them in a heartbeat, but alas, I knew they wouldn't, and it was with a somewhat heavy heart that I took a small pack of three adult diapers to the checkout station.

My heart raced as I stood in the aisle and glanced around to make sure that there was no one around who could recognize me. The last thing I wanted to do was give my colleagues more ammo to make my life difficult. It was a relief to know that the store wasn't busy early during my morning break on Fridays. I reached the cashier quickly, prepared to tell her some story about how I took care of my grandfather on the weekends, but she didn't so much as look my way until it was to tell me what my total came to. The only sound between us was the beep and the sound of her fingers as she keyed that amount into the computer system.

"Of course," I forced out over the lump in my throat as I pulled my card out and handed it to her.

"Would you like a bag with that?" She asked.

"Yes, please," I keyed in my pin. The rustle of plastic announced my exit as the cashier packed my diapers into a bag, and I walked out, trying too hard not to look suspicious.

***

Later that evening, I spent a great deal of time fidgeting in the mirror, convinced that my diaper showed no matter what I wore. Thankfully, the all-caps promise of the adult diapers being *noise-free* and *discreet* seemed to be true enough. I couldn't hear the shifting fabric as I moved. It was the lines I was more concerned with, not to mention the fact that I didn't look like I had an actual butt when I wore jeans. Clothes were strewn all over my bedroom, resembling some kind of closet massacre, evidence of my struggle to find something to wear.

Voices in my head were telling me disapprovingly that I should have bought myself a new dress, but there was one voice insisting that I pull out the clean white box in the bottom of my closet. Gold lettering marked the name of the dress boutique I'd gotten it from, and I traced the curly edges before eventually giving in, tugging the box I hadn't touched since high school out of its hiding spot. Inside was the dress I wore to my senior prom, a dress I only ever wore once, convinced that the feeling of glamor and prettiness that came with it would never be the same on any other night. I told myself that the dress wasn't something I could casually pull off. Now, however, it seemed I had nothing more suitable to wear on my date—an actual date with Connor the Hot Bartender!

When I opened the box, frills and smooth silk was revealed. It was impossible to resist the urge to reach out and touch the soft fabric, brushing my fingertips along the pretty lilac material. Nerves danced through me at the idea of wearing the dress again, but as I pulled it out of the box, unfurling the delicate cloth, my heart soared excitedly. The next thing I knew, it was zipped up my spine, and I was doing small twirls in the mirror. The dress flared at the waist into a waterfall of frills, which meant it didn't cling to the areas where the diaper would be, ended just above the knees, and it was shoulder-less, revealing the barest hint of cleavage beneath my favorite heart pendant. To complete the look, I added an innocent pair of white lace thigh-highs—another item from my high school closet—and a pair of matching wedges. I styled my hair into soft curls and kept my makeup natural.

Before long, it was time to climb into my car to

meet Connor. I typed the address into my GPS, and I was off. He'd texted me the name of the restaurant upon my reluctance to let him pick me up. It was the first date, after all, and I didn't exactly know Mr. Hot Bartender as anything but a bartender. Seeing him outside of the bar was going to be an interesting experience. The thought made my core tighten, and I was pretty sure I was blushing by the time I reached the restaurant. He was probably—and by that, I mean definitely—the most attractive guy I'd ever gone out with. Throw in the kinky stuff, and he was close to being the most attractive guy ever.

***

The restaurant was on the nicer side of town, and it was even fancier on the inside than it was on the outside. There was a stage in the back of the restaurant, and a live band played lowkey jazz music, creating a classic feel when combined with the tasteful décor and candles on every table. As soon as I walked in, I was relieved that I'd decided to wear the prom dress. Cocktail dresses and suits surrounded me. I knew I'd have felt extremely underdressed in anything else that I owned.

A hostess dressed in a figure-hugging crimson dress walked over to me, her hair and makeup was immaculately done to such an extent that I suddenly understood why men struggled to speak when near attractive women. I could barely find the words even after she offered a husky, "Hi, do you have a reservation?"

"I... uh... I think so?" I stammered. She raised her perfectly shaped eyebrows, "Name?"

"Uhm..." I said, looking around.

Oh shit. I don't know what Connor's last name is, I thought to myself, feeling stupid for not knowing.

"Do you have a name?" The hostess repeated, growing impatient.

"The reservation is under Anderson," a deep voice boomed from behind me. I spun around at the same time as the hostess looked up. We were both wearing heels, and Connor was still taller. He looked taller than he had on the other side of the bar. My eyes roved over his entire body, and it was obvious that Connor spent a lot of time in a gym. I wasn't complaining. On the contrary, I nearly had to wipe the corner of my mouth as it watered. Never had I imagined Connor in a suit, but he looked incredibly sexy, and it clung to him in all the right ways.

When Connor gave me a smile, my heart beat a tiny bit faster. His eyes traveling over my body made it worse. I could tell he liked my dress.

"Hey," I murmured in a small voice.

"You're absolutely breathtaking," he wrapped an arm around my waist.

"Ah, Anderson," the hostess said. "Of course. Right this way, please."

We followed her to a private booth near the stage. The lighting was dim, and the space was intimate. Connor and I sat across from one another, and the hostess handed us a menu each. At first, I felt excited and warm about being in such a nice place, but once we were actually seated, all sorts of thoughts and realizations came to mind. For one thing, the awareness that I had a diaper on had all but faded until this particular point of the evening. We were in such a public place, and we weren't here for a normal date. No, we were here to talk about a contract.

I'd done some research on contracts as part of this lifestyle, so I was sure I'd be fine, but what if someone noticed how unusual our meeting was? The idea of being around so many people made me far more nervous than I would have liked to be.

"Could we get a bottle of your finest chardonnay and one strawberry milkshake with a tumbler of vodka and a tumbler of gin?" Connor ordered before the hostess could leave.

"Of course," the hostess gave a tight smile.

"I'll have your waiter bring it over," She said plainly. When she walked away, I turned to Connor.

"I don't think she was happy that you ordered so soon," I whispered.

"Too bad," he shrugged, looking at me intently.

"She's not my concern," Connor replied, taking my hand in his.

"Oh?" I offered. I knew he was talking about me, but I wanted to be sure. He reached into his jacket pocket and pulled out a thin folder.

"I came prepared. Did you?" He said, raising an eyebrow at me. I nodded my head, my tongue darting out to moisten suddenly dry lips, unable to bring myself to confirm with words. He didn't have to elaborate. I knew exactly what he meant, and it made me shift slightly, remembering what I was wearing beneath my dress. I began to flip through the pages of the menu in the hopes that it might distract me. Plus, I was always one of those people who hated ordering, worried I was going to fumble over my own tongue or something. It wasn't exactly what I would call an impossibility, as proven by years of past embarrassing moments.

"Good," he smirked approvingly, opening the folder.

"Now, you've reminded me of something, little one. It has to do with a rule I've put in the contract. Would you like to know what it is?" He said, a wicked gleam in his eye. Did I want to know what it was? My body was buzzing with the anticipation! I nodded my head slowly, trying to keep from showing just how excited and a more than a bit nervous I really was.

"Come over here," Connor inclined his head toward the spot next to him, and I happily shimmied over to the other side of the booth. I was rewarded with, "Good girl." Our drinks arrived then, carried on a tray by a man younger than me, dressed in a crisp tuxedo.

"Your drinks," he said in a suave voice as he set them down. He held the tray up beside his head in a way I'd never seen waiters do outside of film.

"Are you ready to order?" He added after placing our drinks down.

"I am. I'll have the Bouillabaisse," Connor turned to me.

"How about you?" He said, looking at me. I looked between the two of them. My voice caught in my throat. Why did he have to go and put me on the spot like that?

"I... uh..." I stammered. Connor smiled at me and leaned in to whisper in my ear. I nearly lost the ability to speak altogether because his breath was hot, where it tickled the most sensitive part of my neck.

"You know, you could just point, and Daddy will order it for you if you can't pronounce the names, baby girl," he lovingly said. Parts of me I didn't expect to react to such a comment pulsed in response and heat spread out across my chest. Still, I found myself reaching for the menu and pointing out the item.

"She'll have the Coq au vin," Connor turned back to the waiter.

"Thank you," Connor said, dismissing the waiter.

"I'll get right on that," the waiter bowed his head slightly and walked away with absurdly good posture.

"Right," Connor turned back to me.

"Shall we get back to it?" He half-laughed.

"Yes, please," I replied, feeling more overwhelmed than I wish I did.

"Ah! She speaks!" Connor grinned as I shrank into my seat, blushing.

"So, I've made a list I wanna go over with you. We're going to go over some things that you do and don't want as a part of this agreement, and after that, you can tell me if you wanna take a look at the rules I wrote for you to follow," he explained.

"I have to follow rules?" I asked, my eyes widening. I'd read about Daddy Doms giving their Littles rules, but I didn't know how serious Connor was about all this stuff. A lot of the posts referred to fake Daddy Doms, and I had a feeling I was getting the real deal when it came to Connor.

"Mhmm," he hummed.

"So, I want you to tell me if there's anything I should know before we get into this. Are there any health conditions or triggers that you have?" He asked sipping his drink. I just shook my head.

"Okay, we know your experience is

definitely on the beginner side," he said pointing out the obvious. How could I argue? He looked back down at the folder.

"We'll have a safe word too. I'm thinking either *cinnamon* or *pineapple,*" he suggested. "Cinnamon!" I cried out so loudly that several people stared at us. I ducked my head.

"Sorry, I really love cinnamon pancakes," I explained. I thought he would be surprised or even annoyed, but the dimples appeared in his cheeks, and I could tell he was amused.

"Cinnamon, it is," he murmured before continuing, making a quick note in the contract.

"Okay, in that case, I want you to just tick these off for me. We should keep a record because if at a later stage, there are things you want to try or don't want to do anymore, we can simply refer back. You know?" Connor explained as I was busy taking it all in.

"Okay," I took the pen he held out for me, and he slid the folder over. There was an entire checklist of potential acts we could perform, including oral only, soft petting, light sexual activity, and full sexual activity. I looked over at Connor, and if I had any doubts before, his eyes set me at ease. I checked full sexual activity. As I went through the rest of the list, I felt Connor's hand on my inner thigh, slowly edging its way up and beneath my skirt. I bit down on my lower lip as I checked things off. With each tick, Connor's fingers moved further and further up until I could feel his hand against the diaper, and it should have been weird, but it wasn't, not even remotely. No secrets. Non-negotiable. I bit down on my lip. That was a tough one. Check. Diapers. Check. Public display. Well, this was one, wasn't it? Check. Spanking. Check. Collaring. Was that like, ownership? I had seen some cute collars in my research. Check. Connor's hand was so high that my skirt was wrapped around my waist, and his fingertips were already dancing across my waist, teetering around the waistband of the diaper. My heart was racing, and I could barely concentrate on the paper in front of me. Goosebumps rose in the wake of his touch.

"Go on," he whispered. I bit my lip and went back to the list. After all, it didn't seem like Connor was going to take things any further unless I finished. That made sense. It was a contract. What I didn't expect was that I really wanted to see where he was taking things.

Must eat three times a day. That was easy enough. Check. Enforced bedtimes, check. Double-check. Enforced outfits. Check. I wondered if Connor would buy me special Little outfits. I'd already started a wish list: restriction and bondage. I looked over at him, my hand hovering over the checkbox.

"You could always half-tick it, and we know that's a maybe," Connor said.

"I can do that?" I excitedly asked. He nodded his head. With a smile, I half-ticked the checkbox. Soon, I was all done with the main agreements and Connor took the pen so that we could sign it. There was a special signature line for the Little Girl and the Daddy Dom. It struck me at that moment how real what we were doing was. It gave me a thrill, and I found myself moving closer to Connor.

Our meeting was momentarily halted by the arrival of the food. The waiter brought it on a bigger tray, placing our food in front of us. Without another word, he disappeared, and I raised my eyebrows.

"They have weird service here," I said, looking at the fancy meals in front of us.

"These tables are for people who want privacy," Connor explained.

"They won't approach unless absolutely necessary, and when they do, they're discreet," he said before gesturing for me to start my meal.

"Oh. That's a thing?" I asked, curious about how he knew about this type of service. He nodded his head, but the way he was looking at me told me that waiters were the last thing on his mind.

"So, you're officially my Little Girl," Connor said calmly, but I could tell he was impressed with himself. The words ran around my head and in spite of everything, I wanted more than that.

"What... does that mean exactly?" I said, surprised at the speed we were taking things.

"What do you mean?" Connor asked, looking up from his meal.

"Just... well, does being your Little Girl mean? Do we only do what the contract says, or is there more to it?" I asked. Connor leaned in, looking me in the eye.

"Do you want there to be more to it?" He slowly said. Did I? With him so close, I could see the tiny hazel flecks that dotted his eyes, and I found myself wondering how I'd never noticed them before. Years, I'd been going to that bar, and it wasn't as if I'd only ever gone for the drinks. Don't get me wrong, they were amazing, but I'd gone for Connor. I went to talk to him because he was one of the only things that made me smile at the end of a horrible day.

I took a deep breath.

"Yeah, actually. I do," I said more

confidently than I knew I could be. To my surprise, Connor smiled.

"Yeah? Me too," he stated, a smirk of happiness forming in the left-hand side of his mouth. The words brought a smile to my face, and butterflies fluttered in my belly.

"Really?" I almost squealed. Connor took my hand in his free one and squeezed it gently.

"Would you like to be my girlfriend, Jessie Phillips?" Connor formally asked.

"Wait, you know my last name?" I gasped. The corners of his mouth twitched with amusement.

"Believe it or not, I do remember the first day you walked into the bar," he confessed.

"Oh," the tips of my ears went red with heat.

"Right. Yeah, no, I'm gonna go ahead and blame alcohol for my memory loss," I said trying to give myself an excuse. At this, Connor burst out laughing. It was warm and safe and rumbled through his belly.

"You're adorable, but then, you always have been," he said before kissing my cheek.

"I wanna be your girlfriend," I blurted out.

"I can't tell you how happy that makes me, little one," he whispered, squeezing my hand again.

"How about we go through the rules?" He suggested. He handed me a new list. This time, when I took the pen from him, Connor slipped his opposite hand beneath the waistband of the diaper and moved lower and lower until I could feel his fingertips grazing the most sensitive part of my body. I gasped as my clit pulsed in response.

"Keep reading, baby girl," Connor whispered. I only hummed in response, turning back to the list. Some of the rules were repeats of the things I'd checked in the contract, such as enforced outfits when Connor and I were together, and I went into Little Space. My bedtime would be ten p.m. I wasn't allowed to swear. That one made me giggle, but that was cut off as Connor began moving his finger in small, circular motions and it was hard not to moan.

"Yes, I agree to the rules. All of them," I gasped. Biting down on my lower lip, I glanced around to make sure that no one was looking at us and I was surprised to find that they weren't. We were, as Connor had said, in a completely private space. And he was taking full advantage of that because the next thing I knew, one finger was inside me. It wasn't like it had much of a struggle. I wasn't sure that a man had ever made me this excited.

"So wet," Connor murmured approvingly.

"Is my little girl enjoying herself? Does this turn her on?" Connor whispered in my ear.

"Answer me, Jessie," he pressed, moving his finger in and out at an achingly slow pace.

"Does the idea of Daddy fingering your pussy out here in the open, in public, get you all worked up?" He nipped the top of my ear and as he continued to move his finger in and out of me.

"Your pussy certainly likes it. Doesn't it?" He continued. The edge in his voice was enough for me to force out an answer, though it came out breathy and high-pitched.

"Yes," I moaned, rolling my head back as he worked his magic.

"Yes?" He questioned. I looked down at the list. Right at the bottom, I'd already read the very last rule. It was a condition that I had to answer and thank Connor in one specific way.

"Yes, *Daddy*," I whispered.

"There's a good girl," Connor added a second finger and began thrusting them in and out of me much faster than before. I could barely breathe as the pressure in the pit of my belly built and built, taking me higher and threatening to explode.

"Give yourself to me, little one. Show Daddy how much you want him. Do you know how much I want you?" He coaxed as he edged me closer. I shook my head; my curls whipping against my face and clenched my thighs together. My orgasm was within reach, and my hips were moving up to meet Connor's hand, trying to get more of him.

"I want you so much that I'm as hard as a fucking rock right now," he whispered, pressing a kiss to the curve of my neck. With his free hand, he moved mine toward his crotch, and I could feel the obvious bulge through his pants.

"And I can't tell you how much I wish I could bend you over this table to show you what you do to me," he whispered, kissing my cheek.

"Oh, fuck," I gasped. And just like that, Connor's hand was gone. I tried to grab onto it, but Connor was far stronger. I may as well have been a fly for all my efforts.

"Wait! Why?" I complained.

"Because I have to punish you for breaking your first rule," Connor shrugged nonchalantly. His finger still glistened as he reached for a napkin to wipe his hand. As I watched, he closed the folder with the documents signed by both of us and put it back into his jacket before he picked up his knife and fork and began casually eating as if nothing were out of the ordinary.

"Eat your food, little one," he said as if not

moments ago he was about to make me explode. Every part of me wanted to argue, but instead, I settled into my meal. It was an argument I knew I was going to lose. The rules were agreed to only moments before. I shifted uncomfortably for the rest of the meal, pressing my thighs together as if it might provide some form of relief. It was nothing compared to the expert way Connor's fingers danced along my center. I had to admit the food was good, though.

***

After the meal, Connor and I went back to his place. He drove my car because it was easier than having to tell me where he lived. Plus, he had no excuse not to touch me in the passenger seat and boy, did he touch me. My body was tingling from head to toe by the time we reached his house, mostly because all he'd offered were teasing brushes against my breasts and inner thighs, never going further, never touching me the way I really wanted to be touched.

When did I become such a slut? No guy had ever

made me so hot for him before. I barely knew Connor—technically I'd known him for over two years, but this was different—and yet, he could have gotten me to beg for him if he wanted. That's how badly I wanted him.

The moment we got into the house; I was bent over the back of a couch. I barely had a second to take in the house around me. The sound of the door closing was accompanied by the feeling of Connor pressed up behind me. I could feel the bulge in his pants, pressed right against me, with the diaper between us.

"Do you know why I'm punishing you, Jessie?" He asked.

It was so rare for Connor to use my name that I knew I was in trouble.

"Yes, Daddy," I obediently said.

"And why is that?" He asked.

"Because I said the F-word, Daddy," I replied, knowing my mistake. Connor's hands pulled the diaper down, and I felt the cool breeze hit my bare ass. His hands stroked the firm flesh and right when I thought I was okay; he raised one hand and brought it back down. The sound of his hand slapping my butt echoed in the space, and I cried out in both surprise and pain as the heat rushed to the spot. I was sure he'd left a handprint. I didn't have time to linger on the first smack though.

"Count," Connor said. He didn't give me a chance to register what he'd just said before his hand came back down on the other side. I cried out.

"Count!" He growled.
"Two!" I squealed before adding, three, four, five, six, seven." By the time he was done, both my cheeks were red and stinging, but I knew Connor had taken it easy on me because I didn't need to cry, even though I felt awful for having broken a rule. Connor stopped smacking my ass and flipped me around, taking me into his arms. I was breathing heavily, and each movement burned a little.

"I won't break the rule again, Daddy," I said

in a small voice.

"You won't?" He looked down at me, tucking a loose strand behind my ear. My face was warm, and even after I'd been spanked, I closed my eyes and leaned into Connor's gentle touch against my cheek. Connor pulled me into him and held me for a while. I found myself thinking that punishments weren't so bad if this was what followed them. We stayed like that for quite a while, until my ass stopped stinging and I didn't feel so guilty anymore. I was coming back to myself. The next thing I knew, his lips were on mine, and we were kissing. He coaxed my mouth open and drew a moan out of me when his tongue touched my lower lip.

"You took your punishment so well, little one," he finally said when he broke away.

"I'm really proud of you, and I wanted to wait to show you this, but I think you deserve a reward. I have some presents for you," Connor said, his face matching his words.

"Presents?" I clapped my hands together

happily. Connor beamed and walked over to the dining room table. I took in the clean, light, and airy décor. His place was actually really nice and surprisingly neat. I'd have thought a big brawny man like Connor would have lived in a man cave, but it seemed that was not the case. He came back with a gift bag full of gifts for me.

Taking it from him, it was impossible to keep the excitement down. My Little was out in full force, and she had presents! I opened the gift bag and inside was a variety of things, including a fluffy bunny onesie, a coloring book, and a pink pacifier. These were all on my wish list of Little things, and I couldn't believe this was really happening. I didn't think I'd ever been so happy.

"Oh, my gosh, I love them!" I gasped.

"What does my little girl say?" Connor said as he pulled me onto his lap.

"Thank you, Daddy!" I clapped my hands together.

Chapter 4

For the first time in months, I didn't mind being at work. Throughout the day, all I could think about was Connor, and that kept me in a state of hopeful bliss. It was a Friday evening, the first that Connor had off since we'd gotten together. Bartenders apparently never got weekends off, but he had some kind of a surprise for me. Seeing Connor was exciting enough, but I couldn't wait to find out what it was he had planned.

The last time Connor surprised me; he took me on a shopping spree. As a result, I had several new Little outfits that we kept at his house and a few toys. Thus far, we hadn't gotten anything more than that, but getting to wander around dressed like a Little was some of the most fun I'd ever had. The fact that I had someone who could simply let me be while I colored in one of my coloring books was incredible, and I never understood how freeing it would be. Every time I'd wished I were still a child, wished that life was still as simple as it had been back then.

Connor helped show me that it really could be.

"What are you so giddy about?" Lisa asked me the moment I walked into the office, wincing at the sight of me. I simply beamed, ignoring her and headed to my desk. Even Lisa, Queen of all that was bad, couldn't get to me that morning. The day passed by quickly enough with intermittent texts from Connor. He didn't like that we often text while I worked. He said it hindered his good little girl's productivity. When the day ended, Lisa tried to take one last jab at me.

"Are you excited to go home to your life of loneliness? You do know there's more out there than just your bed, right?" She sneered. Gosh, I hated this woman.

"I'll actually be in my boyfriend's bed," I happily sang as I walked out, leaving the office. I didn't look back at her, but I wished I could have seen the look on her face. Little Space and Connor had both instilled a newfound confidence in me, and I felt as if nothing could touch me—not even Lisa. I was still beaming when I got to the car, and by the time I arrived at Connor's house, my cheeks were aching from smiling. Who would have thought?

***

Connor opened the door before I knocked. He was wearing a pair of worn blue jeans that hung off his hips in just the right way and a white T-shirt that was too tight around the biceps, but loose enough that one couldn't quite see all the rippling muscles beneath it. Before I could overthink it, I reached for him, my hands slipping beneath the hem and moving up his sides.

"Uh-huh. Hello to you too," Connor said with a grin.

"Hey, Daddy," I sang, taking my hands out only to run them down over the waistband of his jeans.

"What are we doing tonight?" I added, hoping that I would get want I wanted.

"Now, as much as I wish that was in the

plans," he took both my hands in his, intertwining our fingers.

"I'm taking you out. And I want you to wear one of the outfits Daddy bought for you," he said before kissing my cheek. He stood to the side, and I entered the house, letting go of his hands. "I have to wear one of my outfits out?"

"Mhmm," he nodded.

"Go on. We're gonna be late if you don't get ready soon," Connor said more sternly. I hesitated; my feet glued to the ground. Why did I feel as if I'd been thrown right into the deep end? Suddenly, I wasn't too fond of the idea of a surprise. If I knew where we were going, I could either return to my prior state of bliss or I could say I didn't want to go. Was that too much to ask for?

"Little one," Connor walked over to me. I was surprised to find that he wasn't using his stern voice.

"You're going to love it. Don't you trust Daddy?" He said making me blush. Did I trust Daddy? I wasn't sure I trusted anyone. I mean, it isn't as if the world gave me much reason to trust anything in it. If I had to choose one person, though, it would definitely be Connor.

"Yes, Daddy," I replied, finally making up my mind.

"Good. Now run along," he said, playfully slapping my ass. I raced toward the second bedroom where we kept all my things. It was easier than trying to find space somewhere in Connor's room. I think he liked having a space that was still his. Tugging the chest of drawers open, I was astonished by the sheer amount of stuff that Connor had gotten me. It hadn't all been on our shopping spree. Rather, small things had been added over time, and now I had a great collection. How was I supposed to choose anything to wear? It was our first date all over again. I pulled three onesies out, but I hadn't been out in my pajamas since I was a little girl. I wasn't so sure that I was ready for that one quite yet.

Little by little, I crossed off the outfits that I wasn't willing to wear out in public. Eventually, I ended up with a denim overall and two dresses. Most of the time, dresses were what I wore when I was with Connor. I didn't really want to wear them out. That left the overalls and a cute white T-shirt.

When I walked out with my thumbs beneath the straps and my hair braided into pigtails, Connor looked up from where he sat on the couch and smiled at me. My heart instantly swelled under that gaze. I knew what he was about to say before he said it and it brought a ready smile to my lips.

"Good girl!" Connor exclaimed, his eyes telling me all I needed to know.

***

I was blindfolded the entire way there. I tried to count the turns to figure out where we were going. In the back of my mind, I hoped that we wouldn't be going anywhere familiar. If it was somewhere, I'd been before. I wasn't sure I was going to enjoy this surprise.

Eventually, I had no choice but to give up on figuring it out. Somewhere along the way, I'd miscounted a turn. We could have been in a different city for all I knew. Music played along the drive—an album Connor knew I loved—and I lost all sense of time. Before we arrived, the scent of cake seemed to linger in the air. I shrugged it off, thinking the blindfold must have been messing with my senses. I was just hungry, and my nose imagined what my belly craved.

If I thought Connor would remove my blindfold when we got there, I was wrong. Once we arrived, he parked and came around to lift me out of the car. Then, like some kind of newlywed couple, he carried me toward the place, and only afterward did he finally take my blindfold off.

"You ready?" He asked before untying it. I nodded my head excitedly, and I could see at long last. Lucky for me, the light was dim, and it didn't hurt my eyes as they adjusted to it. The first colors to hit my retina were pink and purple. Everywhere I looked, the pastel colors that Littles seemed to be so fond of hit me. There were too many other women—no, girls—to count, all of them dressed in Little outfits. Lace, pastels, and innocence speckled the room. Even so though, there were a few who were darker shadows in the space, as cute and Little as the rest. I didn't even know there was such a thing as a Little who expressed their happiness through the color black but seeing the diversity all around me made my heart feel light. The corners of the room, painted in a sweet pattern of pinks and whites, were packed with hundreds of stuffies. Off to the distance, I could see several other Littles having tea parties or playing with dolls in forts. It looked better than any play place I'd ever visited as a kid, and I was ecstatic. I knew I was deep in Little Space, and this place was the biggest trigger. The words Connor said before all this started came to mind, the way he knew exactly what a 'Little Girl' such as myself needed. Out of the corner of my eye, I knew Connor was happy with my response, but I had more important concerns.

"Daddy, can I please go play?" I said, practically hopping up and down.

"Sure, little one. But remember that this

isn't the only room," He explained. I'd been ready to run off, but I stopped at the sound of that.

"There are other rooms?" I asked, curious about what I would learn tonight.

"Of course. There are play sessions happening, spa sessions, and plenty of different aged rooms," Connor continued to explain.

"That's so cool," I breathed, my eyes wide as saucers.

"Do you wanna take a walk through them?" Connor asked, taking my hand in his. At that, I froze for the first time. The rooms were interesting enough, but I didn't want to walk through them right now. There was a table with a group of three girls coloring, and every part of me wanted to be there with them. I knew this was a judgment-free zone. I could always go look around later. I shook my head, my pigtails flying.

"I wanna go color," I said, biting my bottom lip. Connor's mouth twitched, but he didn't quite smile even though I could see the joy in his eyes.

"Okay, go have fun. I'm gonna go get us

something to eat," he said turning on his heel. I looked over at the table of food. There was cake. Without wasting another moment, I moved toward the coloring table as quickly as I possibly could. The three other girls looked up as I approached, and at the sight of one of them, my heart sank to the pit of my stomach. The blood drained from my face, and it felt as if the temperature had been turned down to sub-zero. I knew one of those faces. Lisa.

Chapter 5

"Oh, what do we have here?" Lisa stood from the table, wearing a frilly white dress paired with pink thigh-highs and a pink collar. My mouth was suddenly dry.

"Little Jessie. This is too precious," she said, delight in her eyes. I could barely move as Lisa walked around me, taking in my outfit with a smug look on her face.

"Wh... what are you doing here?" I stammered.

"Come on, Little Jessie," Lisa rolled her eyes.

"I know you're not that stupid. I'm here for the same reason as you. I just, you know, do it better. But that's nothing new, is it?" She said smirking at me. My happiness was dashed in mere moments. Of all the people to be here, to find out about my secret, why did it have to be her? I hated Lisa with a passion, and she knew it because I was pretty sure she hated me just as much. And based on the way Lisa's eyes were glittering with malice, I'd have hazarded a guess that she definitely wasn't willing to change her ways because she found out we were both Littles. On the contrary, I had a feeling that things were about to get so much worse.

"Is this really the best you could do?" Lisa suddenly asked. She reached out to take the tip of one of my pigtails, grimacing.

"How tacky," she spat out at me. Looking around, I knew I wasn't the only girl with braided pigtails. Lisa was just trying to get to me. I wished it wasn't working. At the coloring table, the other two girls were watching us with wide eyes, their coloring pencils still in hand.

"I know!" Lisa clapped her hands together.

"How about you let me do your hair, Jessie? I bet I could make it look really pretty, better than the mess it is right now. And you should totally take off your clothes," she said, making me nervous.

"Excuse me?" I asked, backing away as she

tried to untie one of the pink ribbons in my hair.

"Yeah, there are rooms where you're allowed to do that. Playrooms, you know?" She gave me an evil grin. As sweet as her voice sounded, my instincts were on red alert. It was too sickly sweet.

"I could show you," she said, getting aggressive.

"No thanks," I shook my head, turning away. As I did, Lisa grabbed hold of one of my braids and yanked me back. I cried out in pain, and both the other girls at the table jumped upward, trying to pull Lisa off of me. She was stronger than she looked, and she refused to let go. My eyes were stinging with pain, and I shut them tightly. The last thing I wanted to do was let Lisa see me cry.

"Hey! Let go of her!" Connor's voice rang out. Suddenly, my hair was released, and I felt the strong arms of my Daddy as he wrapped them around me, pulling me to him. I opened my eyes, expecting to see his eyes filled with worry, but that didn't happen. Instead, Connor was staring at Lisa as if he'd seen a ghost. When I glanced over at her, Lisa had a similar expression on her face.

"Wait," Lisa murmured in a small voice.

"You're Jessie's Daddy?" Lisa said, almost choking on the words. Oh, no, no, no, no. It was obvious. They knew each other. I wasn't the only one who knew Lisa. Even worse than that, they knew each other in these circles. My mind raced, and I was putting puzzle pieces together that I hoped didn't fit. But then Connor spoke in a stern voice that I recognized from the few times I'd been punished and reprimanded.

"What the hell is wrong with you, Lisa? I'm ordering you to leave Jessie alone. Don't come anywhere near her," Connor growled. The smallness disappeared, and Lisa's face twisted into a sneer.

"You can't tell me what to do anymore!" She confirmed my fears as she looked over at me with a toothy smile.

"You've already downgraded," she said looking me up and down. I couldn't stop the tears from falling. They fell with the freedom of a child, hot and relentless, dripping down my face and off of my chin. That was the thing I'd discovered about Little Space; the more comfortable I grew with myself and that mindset, the easier I fell into its trap which was that it was hard to pull myself out. I dropped to the floor and cried like an absolute baby even though there were several people watching us at this point, watching me sob.

Lisa gave a girly giggle, sitting back down at the table and picking up her pencil as if nothing had happened. She was blurry through my tears, but I wanted to throw something at her. Before I could, I felt Connor's arms around me. He lifted me up—he carried me around a lot in Little Space—and took me over to the food table.

"Hey," he whispered gently, pressing a kiss to my forehead. He got down on his haunches in front of me, reminding me once again how small I was compared to him, and held my hands.

"This isn't exactly how I pictured your first play party. There were so many things I wanted to show you. But Daddy will understand completely if you want to leave," he lovingly said. I glanced over my shoulder. That was a mistake. Lisa was watching, and she stuck her tongue out at me like the snake she was. I swiped at tears and whimpered, "I don't think I can stay, Daddy."

"Okay," Connor nodded. I could tell he was disappointed, but he pulled me in and stroked my hair.

"I'm sorry things turned out this way, sweetheart," he gently said, taking my hand in his. With that, Connor led me out of the play party. There were still eyes on us, but I knew what it was like to be a Little. They would all go back to their fun in no time. I might be the talk when they left and went back to their normal lives, but for now, there were more interesting things than the crying girl in overalls. Connor squeezed my hand gently every so often to let me know he was there and when we got into the car, he didn't let go the whole way home.

"I wish I'd gotten a piece of cake," I

mumbled sadly, staring out of the window.

***

The following day, as much as I would have liked to stay in bed with Connor's warm arms wrapped around me, I couldn't. But that didn't mean I hopped out of bed, happy to get to my day. My bunny slippers—another gift from Connor—dragged along the floor as I went to get ready. I was lucky enough that Connor was a morning person, which only made me wonder what on earth he was doing with me, as he made coffee and breakfast. How I would have gotten through the day without coffee was beyond me. I certainly hadn't had the time to make it, given the fact that I hit the snooze button on my alarm one too many times.

On the drive to work, I hoped that Lisa wasn't on the same shift as me, mostly because I was wearing a dress. It was the only option at Connor's, but it was less girly than my others; a simple white dress that flared at the waist and ended halfway down my knees, something Connor and I agreed was better for when I wore diapers, which was admittedly quite often. Nevertheless, wearing dresses to work was not something I normally did. My emotions were tangled. Every time I closed my eyes, I could see Lisa's sneer burned into the back of my eyelids. Vulnerability charged through me, and I couldn't help feeling disgusted, as if something were crawling along my skin. Lisa used to be Connor's Little! For a brief moment, I had thought I was special, but I no longer felt that way. Tears threatened to fall again, and I wished that I could call in sick. It wouldn't have been a complete lie. The thought of Lisa and her perfect face, a face I wanted to punch, was enough to make my stomach turn violently.

As much as I wanted to be, I couldn't be mad at Connor. It wasn't as if I'd been a part of his life. I was nothing more than the girl behind the bar. Still, the thought stung. Why did it have to be Lisa? My hope for a quiet morning was dashed as I heard Lisa's greeting chime the moment I sat down in my cubicle. It made me squirm uncomfortably. I glanced out to see her in a dress that showed off all her curves and had a swooping neckline.

I forced myself to look away and focus on my computer screen. There were more important things to do. I wasn't at work for Lisa, after all. And yet, it seemed as if Lisa might be at work for me. She peered over the top of my cubicle, and I knew this wasn't going to be good. Lisa looked like a bitch with unfinished business.

"Isn't it a beautiful day? You should wear dresses more often, Little Jessie. It suits you," Lisa said in the velvet way she spoke. Ignoring her, I opened another email, my heart hammering.

"Little Jessie," she continued, looking around conspiratorially as if we would ever be co-conspirators.

"Are you and your Daddy going to the next play party?" She continued making me want to punch her in the face.

"That's what I thought," Lisa smiled and walked around, entering my tiny cubicle. I was speechless as she sat back on the limited desk space I had. Her long, tanned legs annoyed me compared to my own short, pale ones.

"I think we can have some fun here. You see, from now on, I'm in charge around here. You're gonna do everything I tell you because if you don't, well, let's just say I'm not so sure I can keep my mouth shut about all the *little* things you've been getting up to lately," she said making me shake my head in despair. The double-meaning didn't escape my notice, and my heart pounded faster than before.

"Why are you doing this, Lisa?" I said, the words coming out more pathetic than I had wished.

"That's not important," she hissed, and for a second, I imagined her as a real snake, flinching.

"Don't even think about saying a word to Connor. If you do, I'll know, and I will make things worse for you," she said as she fidgeted with one of the files on my desk.

"I wonder how the execs would feel about

you bringing your private life to work with you," making me blush. My eyes widened.

"What are you talking about?" I said trying to gain some control. Lisa smirked and stretched her leg out to lift the front of my skirt. I pushed back from the desk, escaping her and stood up indignantly. Before I could raise my voice, scream at her like I wanted, she laughed.

"I can see your diaper," Lisa remarked snidely. While I spluttered, heat rushing through my entire body instead of just my cheeks, Lisa shimmied gracefully out of the small space.

Chapter 6

I had the weekend off. It was rare that I had two consecutive days off, much less an entire weekend. Connor took the weekend off because of it, and he was arriving at my house at any moment. I was ready and packed, slumped on my sofa. I had nothing better to do. Normally, I'd have been running around getting things ready at the last minute, but since I'd had such trouble sleeping lately, I'd spent most of the night packing. I'd showered and dressed hours before a text beeped on my phone to let me know that Connor was on the way.

Things with Connor and I had been rocky lately. I got the feeling that he was avoiding me, much to my dismay. One would have thought me being all over him all the time would have been something he enjoyed, but no. Apparently sitting on my knees and waiting for Daddy to get home from work so that I could give him pleasure was cause for concern.

I sighed, rolling my eyes at the memory of Connor's face. I'd expected him to be happy, but he'd gotten down on his knees and asked me if I was okay. Of course, I wasn't okay. Could I tell him that? Of course not.

Perhaps it was the suddenness that got to him. After all, he probably expected me to distance myself after what happened with Lisa. I couldn't though. The only thing that took my mind off of it was Connor and being with Connor. I knew it was wrong, but right now, I didn't know how else to cope.

Things had gotten so much worse at work, and I had no idea what to do anymore. I didn't want to stop being who I was, especially now that I'd figured out who that was, and I still had to follow the rules Connor laid out for me. That meant I was following two different sets of rules because Lisa had a set of her own, designed to torture me. For one thing, Connor's rule was that I wear diapers at all times. How did Lisa counteract this? She wanted me to wear dresses to work at least three times a week. I could be grateful that she didn't make it every day, but I knew she didn't do that for me. I was bound to get strange looks if I walked into the office on the days when we had meetings wearing one of my Little dresses, and it seemed Lisa was having too much fun with me to put a stop to it quite yet.

Outside, I heard Connor's car arrive, followed by the horn. I got up and took my bags with me, heading over to the door. I opened it to find Connor with his hand up, ready to knock on the spot above my head. His mouth dropped open at the sight of me—and my bags.

"This has got to be some kind of miracle. You're actually on time," he said with a smile.

"Well, that's totally uncalled for," I dragged my suitcase behind me, ignoring his offered hand as he tried to take the bag.

"Oh, come on, little one. I was only joking," Connor said, kissing the top of my head. We'd already reached the car, and he popped open the trunk. This time I let him take my suitcase because there was no way I could lift it on my own. My lower lip was pushed out into a pout that I could tell Connor enjoyed far too much.

"You're supposed to comfort me, not look at me like I'm adorable," I said, pouting at him. Connor just grinned.

"But you are adorable," he said, shrugging his shoulders.

"Daddyyy," I whined.

"Okay, okay," he held up his hands in surrender. I knew we were only playing around, but when Connor's eyes crinkled in concern, I wanted to dive under the car and hide away forever.

"Get in the car. We've got to get to the hotel before check-in closes," he said.

"Well, don't look at me. I'm on time," I was already at my door and climbing into the car.

"Watch your attitude, little lady!" Connor called, walking around to the driver's side.

My core tightened at the strict tone of voice. I

couldn't help it. Lately, I'd grown more and more bratty. I had a feeling it was the idea of Connor punishing me that did it. As he buckled up and the engine purred to life, I reached into his lap and ran my small hand over the crotch of his jeans.

"Jessie," he murmured warningly. I ignored him, and as we pulled into the road, I unzipped his jeans.

"Jessie, behave yourself," Connor warned.

"Where's the fun in that?" I smirked, reaching in and freeing his cock. It was already hard.

"Besides, you can't exactly say you don't like it," I teased.

"That's beside the point. I'm telling you to behave. If you don't, you're not going to have a very good time on this vacation," he said. I didn't listen to him. My hand was wrapped around his thick shaft, stroking up and down. As angry as he sounded, Connor's breathing had quickened, and his cock was harder than ever. In the hopes that I could assuage him, I leaned across the seat and wrapped my mouth around the tip. It was warm, and I could already taste the precum as I began bobbing my head up and down. There was nothing Connor could do about it—or so I thought. He turned off the next chance he got, pulled over, and turned the engine off. My heart skipped a beat.

"If you don't sit back in your seat and behave, we'll turn around, and you won't see me until next weekend," he said. I immediately pulled off and sat back in my seat, staring at him with wide eyes.

"You wouldn't do that," I gasped.

"Try me," he growled. His jaw was clenched, and I could see a muscle twitching in his cheek. The anger in his eyes was real.

"Rules are rules. And don't think I'm not going to punish you the second we check-in," he sternly said. Swallowing the lump that formed in my throat, I squirmed in my seat.

"Yes, Daddy," I said, my voice came out as barely a whisper. He didn't answer me as he started the car, didn't even look at me as we headed back out onto the road. The rest of the drive was achingly silent. I wanted to put some music on, but I didn't dare move. I'd never seen Connor so angry with me, and I didn't want to push my luck any more than I already had.

***

As soon as we got to the hotel, we changed into our bathing suits. Connor had calmed down immensely, and I was relieved that my butt wouldn't be subject to his wrath. The whole point of the trip was that we could take a special "grown-up" vacation together and we had a couple's massage, facials, and zip-lining on our list of planned activities. I didn't want anything to spoil it.

The only problem was that my phone had vibrated three times since we arrived, and I knew whose messages I'd find if I checked it. It was on silent after the third text from Lisa asking me how my weekend with Daddy was going. My mood was worse than ever. Wasn't it bad enough that she tortured me at work? Did she have to do it on my days off too? What did she even get out of it?

"Jessie?" Connor broke into my thoughts. I looked over at him standing in the doorway of the bathroom, wearing nothing but a towel around his waist, and instantly knew I hadn't been responsive for a while.

"Are you all right, baby girl?" He was clearly concerned.

"I'm fine, Daddy," I said absently.

"You know," he came toward me, and there was a different tone in his voice.

"I think I know something that'll cheer you up," he said. He had that look in his eye again, that hungry one that made me feel like prey, and I could already feel moisture pooling between my legs. I had a tiny pink bikini on, and it couldn't defend against Connor's hands and his mouth. His hand was between my legs, stroking over the bikini bottoms, and his mouth was on my left nipple over the bikini top.
Under his attention, my nipples grew hard, and goosebumps rose on my skin. Every tiny touch

seemed to send a charge of sensation straight to my center, where his fingers were manipulating me in circles. My mouth fell open in a moan as Connor shifted the bathing suit bottoms to the side, giving him full access to my pussy. I knew for a fact that those bottoms had a wet spot on them, but that was irrelevant because all that mattered was that Connor was touching me and my body was singing with pleasure.

Connor broke away from my breasts only to press his lips to mine, eliciting another moan. I kissed him back fervently, but Connor seemed to be playing the slow game. For every advance I made, he took a figurative step back, frustrating me to no end.

"Daddy," I eventually whined, breaking away from his mouth. I reached behind me and pulled on the knot holding my top together, allowing it to fall and leaving my breasts exposed to Connor's eyes, heaving with my breaths.

"I want you..." I said, giving him my best puppy dog eyes. The towel around his waist had a tent in it, and I reached out to unhook it, revealing Connor's erection. My mouth watered at the sight alone. There was no way he could hide that he wanted me too, so why was he teasing me?

Making love to Connor was the only thing that kept my mind off Lisa. Every other torturous second, I could see her smug face, and it made me angry. I knew I was probably becoming a bit much, but I didn't care. Connor's cock and attention were my distraction, my medicine. I didn't think it was so wrong of me to want my boyfriend as much as I did, especially if it kept me sane.

Connor sensed my urgency. He picked me up so suddenly that I squealed in surprise, promptly giggling as he walked us backward toward the bed. He sat down and positioned me on his lap. Without removing my pink bikini bottoms, Connor lined himself up with my entrance and sat me down on his shaft. We both sighed in pleasure as he filled me up.

I leaned in to kiss him again, whispering against his lips.

"Thank you, Daddy," I softly said. Normally, that would have been enough to set him off, but not this time. Connor turned into a primal animal whenever I called him Daddy while we had sex. For some reason, today was different.

"Do you know how special you are to me, little one?" He whispered as he began to rock his hips, gliding slowly in and out of me. His fingers were digging into the soft flesh of my butt, aiding him in his thrusts as he lifted and dropped me onto his cock in time with them.

"You mean so much to me," he said looking at me lovingly. My heart hammered in my chest and in spite of myself, my walls clenched and convulsed around his length. With each word he said, I got hotter and hotter. I loved the rough sex and being taken, but this was an entirely new experience, and I didn't know how to react to it. My body, on the other hand, was deeply enjoying itself. I could only moan in response.
Tightening my thighs around his waist, I tried to leverage myself to ride him faster and harder, but

Connor had a firm grip on me, and he was taking charge. I was close to my orgasm, could feel it building with every delicious stroke of his dick inside me, but I wasn't close enough. I wanted to go over the edge. I wanted the earth to shatter around me. I wanted him to keep moving against that spot until I became a writhing mess.

"Please," I finally whimpered.

"Please fuck me harder, Daddy. Please," I begged. I could see the shock on his face—after all, that should have been grounds for punishment— but Connor didn't stop. He flipped me onto my back beneath his huge muscular body and began driving into me with abandon. I threw my head back and dug my nails into his strong shoulders, my legs open as wide as they could be.

"Is this what you want?" Connor growled down at me.

"You want to be used like a little slut? That's what my little girl wants?" He said, thumping into my pussy.

"Oh, God," I moaned again and again. His

words did things to me, and he was hitting that spot every single time he thrust home. I could feel it getting nearer, and I shut my eyes, my breaths coming out in high-pitched whimpers as Connor took me. I could tell he was close too, could feel it in the erratic movements of his hips. And finally, when I felt the heat of him shooting into me, I let go in a loud cry, exploding around him and writhing beneath him.

When Connor finally pulled back from me, he heaved a sigh. I knew he was frustrated—most likely with me—but I didn't know how to help that. This was not the bliss I was used to basking in after Connor took me. I made the mistake of making it worse than it already was by reaching for my phone on the nightstand.

On Monday, I want you to wear the shortest dress you own. I suggest you learn to squat when you need to pick something up. I wouldn't want you to reveal your diaper or anything. You know how clumsy I am.

I huffed and slammed the phone back down on the

nightstand. It was all I could do not to throw it across the room. The action caught Connor's notice.

"Jessie, that's it. I'm trying really hard here. I know you need your privacy, but I'm putting my foot down. I want you to tell me what's going on," he said.

"Nothing's going on," I lied, crossing my arms over my chest, fighting while naked brought a whole other level of vulnerability with it.

"I'm serious. Tell me. You know the rules," he said, trying to be patient.

"Fuck the rules!" I cried out. Connor stared at me for a full minute before he pointed to the corner of the room.

"Time out. Stand in the corner," he shouted pointing to the particular corner which took his fancy.

"Oh, so now you wanna punish me?" I spat back, tears hot in my eyes. He gritted his teeth.

"We'll talk when you're ready to tell me what's really been going on," he said shaking his head.

"That'll be never," I snapped. Nevertheless, I listened to his orders and walked over to the corner with my head down. I stood with my hands behind my back. My throat constricted the way it did when I cried. Disappointing my Daddy wasn't something I ever wanted to do. At that moment, I hated Lisa with every fiber in my body.

Chapter 7

On Monday, I showed up to work wearing the dress Lisa told me to wear. The moment I got to the office, I knew I'd probably made what could be one of the biggest mistakes in my life. Balloons were hanging from the ceiling, a gathering of my colleagues dressed far better than they usually dressed, and tables on tables of food and drink. It was a work function.

The worst part was that I'd known there was a work function coming up, purely because I'd been trying my best to get out of it. Unfortunately, it was compulsory for everyone to attend. The weekend had been so distracting that I completely forgot about the function altogether, forgot about every plan I'd had in place to ensure that Lisa didn't entrap me. Now, I was wearing one of my Little outfits, carrying the bag that I took over to Connor's house when I visited, and a diaper beneath my skirt. Panic struck me, and I immediately made my way toward my cubicle to hide, keeping my head down even as people tried to greet me.

I wished I'd brought Connor along. He was my anchor. I knew if anyone would be able to protect me, it would be him. Honestly, all he had to do was stand beside me, and no one would dare approach the giant, lest he grind their bones for his morning toast or something equally ridiculous. Alas, Connor wasn't here, and I was on my own.

"Well, look at you!" An excited voice suddenly cried out. Lisa raced toward me, wearing a fishtail dress that went all the way down her long legs and made her look more like an hourglass than usual. She looked glamorous and chic, whereas I looked like a cupcake.

"Oh, Little Jessie, I looove that dress on you. We're going to have so much fun!" Lisa said clapping her slender hands together. I wanted to swear at her, but my ass still stung from the weekend. Connor had put me in my place several times while we were at the hotel. I had to admit that eventually, my attitude calmed down, I calmed down, and by the end of the vacation, I was feeling a lot better. The aftercare, being held by my Daddy, turned out to be what I really needed. You know, aside from telling him the truth and letting him give me advice on how to deal with it.

"I take it you kept to our agreement," Lisa said sternly as if she could read my mind. "Connor won't be turning up tonight?" She sneered.

"Connor doesn't know anything about how horrible you are if that's what you're asking, Lisa," I said. She gave a giggle, girlish and falsely sincere.

"Good. That's the way I like it. Now run along and get coffee for me, will you? You know how I like it," she simply said. With that, she rejoined the party on the other side of the office, sashaying in between a group of men and dancing to the music as it played. All eyes were on her, including mine. I made my way toward the kitchen and made her a cup of coffee, exactly the way she liked it. Lisa had some kind of magical extra sense that made it impossible to spike her drink or even spit in it. She would know. I already tried.

The sound of the kettle boiling helped. It was white noise, blocking out the sounds of the function. In all honesty, even if Lisa wasn't torturing and blackmailing me, I wouldn't have enjoyed the function. I never had before. The firm wasn't exactly my idea of fun. It was stifling, and it blocked any sense of creativity I might have had. It's probably why my favorite pastime as a Little was to color. I'd always loved art.

With a click of the kettle, I poured the water into Lisa's special cup, a cup no one in the office ever drank from if they wanted to keep their jobs and added some creamer before reluctantly rejoining the function.

Lisa was easy enough to spot. All one had to do was look for the group of men huddled in one particular area. She'd be in the middle of them, showered with the attention of men who all wanted to sleep with her. I didn't know why they bothered. It was obvious to me that she would never give them the time of day.

"Here you go, Lisa," I called, making my way through the gap. This was one of Lisa's rules. No matter what she was doing, I was to follow through on what she'd asked me to do. It was her way of making sure I got the attention I desperately wanted to avoid.

"Your coffee," I meekly said. I froze in my tracks when I saw Lisa. She had my backpack strapped to her shoulders; the overnight bag I was meant to be taking to Connor's later that night. The men were all chuckling as she twirled round and round with it, making fun of its rainbow colors. My breath hitched.

"What are you doing?" I demanded.

"Oh, there you are, Little Jessie!" Lisa clapped her hands.

"I was just showing off your bag. The boys think that I should have it. Don't you, boys?" She said with her snake eyes looking at me.

"Hear, hear!" The cry was accompanied by the scent of alcohol. The men had been drinking punch for quite some time.

"That's not funny," I said, moving deeper into the huddle.

"Give it back," I added quickly.

"But I don't want to," Lisa hissed.

"I don't care what you want, Lisa! It's my bag," I yelled. I could feel my blood being to boil. Lisa's eyes darkened, the blue flashing as she glared at me.

"Is that so? Well, Jessie, I want you to back down. This is my bag now," she teased.

"No, Lisa, it isn't," I said glaring at her. The men were no longer laughing, but the stupid pop songs that Lisa loved to listen to were still playing in the background. I knew she was in charge of the playlist because I could hear this very same playlist coming from her earphones whenever she left work early. They were songs that I might have liked if not for their connection to Lisa. As it was, they only added fuel to the fiery rage I felt simmering within me.

There was no mistaking the look in Lisa's eyes. She

wanted me to back down, wanted me to submit to her will as I had been, but I was too angry. Lisa had finally crossed a line. If it weren't for her, nothing would be wrong in my relationship, and I was tired of feeling so worn down. If it weren't for her, I would have had a better weekend, one without tears. If it weren't for her, my experiences as a Little would have been a hundred times better. I tried to figure out what would happen if I didn't back down. What could Lisa do? It wasn't as if she could simply out me. Most people didn't even understand what a Little or a Daddy Dom was. I would know since I'd been a part of that majority several months ago.

"Are you sure you wanna do this?" Lisa asked, arching one of her perfect brows at me the way she always did when she was testing my will.

"Give me my bag," I said, this time, I wasn't going to break.

Lisa's face broke into a grin that made my heart skip a beat.

"Don't say I didn't warn you," Lisa said shrugging

her shoulders. In one swift move, Lisa ripped my backpack off her shoulders and unzipped the top compartment.

"No!" I screamed, diving for her.

The coffee landed on the floor, hot and steaming. Men jumped away from us as I knocked Lisa to the ground, reaching for my bag. Lisa managed to hold it out of my reach until I grabbed a handful of her long blonde hair, recalling the way she'd tugged at my pigtails at the play party. She grunted in pain and knocked her elbow back, hitting me right beneath my ribs. The sting and force threw both the breath and the strength out of me.

"Stop it!" Someone cried out.

"What the hell is going on here?" Another added. We didn't hear them. We were too occupied with our fight for my backpack. Despite their protests, no one intervened.

Lisa took the opportunity to push me off onto my back on the ground. One hand clutched my side as I tried to catch my breath, and that's when she took her chance. I could only watch on in horror, crying out for her to stop. Lisa turned my backpack upside down and began shaking it until one by one. The contents fell onto the ground.

The first thing to fall was a notebook and pen, the second thing a packet of coloring pencils, and that was followed by my coloring book. If that wasn't bad enough, I already knew what was coming next. I knew Lisa wouldn't stop until every last item was out for everyone to see. She giggled and laughed so hard that mascara streaks ran down her high cheekbones. I stood from the ground, wishing I could kick her in the face, in the same second that one of my adult diapers and a pink paci landed on the floor of the office.

I shouldn't have even bothered trying to cover it up, but that didn't stop me from diving for it. Lisa's malicious laugh rang out above me, and once she started laughing, everyone started laughing. That's when I realized my skirt had lifted in the fight. It didn't matter that I tried to cover up the coloring book, paci, or diaper. Everyone had already seen mine, covered in tiny stickers of butterflies that

Connor had bought for me to make them prettier.

"Oh, my God. This is even better than I imagined it would be," Lisa said through laughter. Maybe if I didn't have people laughing at me from every direction, I might have stood up and punched her.

Instead, I gathered all my things and shoved them back into my bag as quickly as I could. I didn't even bother zipping it up before I hightailed it out of there. The sound of laughter followed me all the way into my car, echoing in my ears as I started the engine and made my way home.

***

Tears rolled down my cheeks as I answered the phone.

"Jessie? Are you still at work?" His voice was like butter.

"No, I'm not," I sobbed.

"What happened? What's going on? Are you okay?" He said, as he bombarded me with questions before I had the chance to answer, not that I knew how to answer. For a second, I forgot he couldn't see me shaking my head on the other side of the phone. I pulled the covers over my body, hiding from the world.

"Jessie, please talk to me. Please," he said, concern in his voice.

"Lisa emptied my bag in front of everyone at work. They all saw my diaper and other stuff," I cried.

"She did *what.* That fucking—"?!" Connor yelled, making me flinch.

"I'm fine," I interrupted.

"Do you want me to come over? I can bring food. And a movie," he said. I loved that he was trying.

"No, please don't. Don't come over. Not tonight," I said, deciding it was better to be alone.

"Jessie..." His voice was low, and I could almost see him running his hands through his hair.

"Please. I want to be alone. I just want to be alone," I said. He sighed, blowing static into my ear. When he spoke again, the anger had all but gone. His voice was gentle.

"I'll be here when you're ready to come back to me, baby girl," he said before hanging up the phone.

Chapter 8

I'd long since succumbed to the numbness that echoed throughout every part of my body. I couldn't feel anything. I lay in bed, lifeless, and disconnected from the world. It was a world I wanted nothing to do with anyway. It was cruel, and so were the people in it.

Lisa was the one who broke me and ruined my life, but somehow, I couldn't stop thinking about all the people in the world who were exactly like her. There were so many, and in the terrible state of mind I found myself in, I lingered on them. Needless to say, it didn't exactly improve my mood or state of mind. On the contrary, I sank into a pit of despair where I wondered what exactly the point of ever leaving the house again would be.

I hadn't been back to work since Lisa exposed me in front of all those people. The memory of their faces, all of my colleague's judgmental faces, was enough of a deterrent. Alongside my fear that they might look at me that way again, might never stop looking at me that way, it was the thought that they could do worse things that kept me at bay. After all, there was no telling how many of them were like Lisa. If she could empty my bag out like that, who was to say others wouldn't behave the same way?

I wasn't sure how long it had been since the event, but I wouldn't have been surprised if several days had passed. It felt as though I'd been drowning in my shame for years. Nevertheless, I'd begun to think about what I could be missing. Withdrawing from the world that hurt me seemed like a good idea at the time. Unfortunately, I knew that I would have to emerge from my blankets eventually.

Connor invaded my thoughts. I couldn't stop thinking about how angry he'd been the last time he called. The anger hadn't been directed at me, and though I didn't think it at the time, it was kind of sweet how he wanted to stand up for me.

At the thought of climbing out of bed, every single

bone in my body ached, but I knew I had to do it. I'd made up my mind. I could only stand to wallow in my own self-pity for so long. I threw the duvet off of me as if ripping a bandage off of a fresh wound.

Somehow, I immediately felt better. I didn't realize how hot I was until I felt the cool air on my legs.

I decided to take small, slow steps, treating myself as I would a scared, rescued kitten beginning to trust the world again. If I moved too quickly, took in too much, I might run back to my hiding place. I calmly sat myself up, and one by one swung my legs to the side of the bed. I sat there for a moment, taking in deep slow breaths.

My chest was tight and sore. It felt like this was the first time I was breathing since my withdrawal, and only now did I realize how thick and stuffy the air in my room actually was. I needed to open the windows or something, along with change the sheets. It was dark and stuffy in my room. I think I closed the curtains the day I got home from the function, and they'd been closed since.

I knew that I'd been dramatic over the past several days, but I felt like I had the right to be, given the circumstances.

Forcing myself to stand up, I made my way over to the curtains. My hands moved mechanically, flinging the curtains open before I had the chance to rethink my decision. I narrowed my eyes and prepared to be blinded by the bright sunlight flooding into my room. That didn't happen. It was actually grey and cloudy outside. A short snort escaped as I considered the fact that the world was sulking along with me.

Opening the windows and breathing in the wonderful smell of rain to come, I felt just a tiny bit better than before, despite having felt as though I would never feel good again only moments before. The only things left to do were brush my teeth, wash my body, and try to get rid of the smell stinking up my room. Part of me thought that smell might just be me.

I wasn't ready to rejoin the world, but a shower

was well overdue. My phone rang as I made my way to the bathroom, and I paused for a moment, thinking about answering it. My phone had been ringing non-stop since the function. I was worried that if I picked it up, it would be someone I didn't want to talk to. The mere thought of seeing a name I didn't want to see kept me away.

More than anything, I thought if it was Connor, I wouldn't be able to ignore it. Not knowing who was calling or why was the safest option. So, naturally, I decided to ignore it again.

My phone rang several more times while I was in the shower, but I was too busy enjoying the hot water cascading down my skin, and the smell of fruity scents of my body wash and shampoo. I didn't care if it was ringing or not.

Once my body was clean, I simply stood beneath the running water and breathed in the steam. It was amazing how therapeutic showers could be. People often overlooked that, myself included. Then again, it wasn't as if I could spend all day in a shower. Otherwise, that's probably how my last few days would have played out, rather than reducing myself to the lump under the bed covers.

Eventually, I jumped out of the shower. Getting dried and dressed was relatively easy, apart from the fact that my muscles ached with lack of use. I thought I might have wanted to jump right back into bed but seeing at how dirty and messed up it looked made me want to throw it all in the wash instead. I walked past my phone on the way to the washing machine and heard a single message tone go off.

It made me pause for a moment. Answering a phone call was something I was completely against at this stage, but how bad could looking at a message be? Odds were there were several waiting for me. If it was from Connor, I might be inclined to answer him, but at least I wouldn't have to talk to him. I didn't think I could handle hearing his voice yet. The anger I'd heard still haunted me.

In the end, my curiosity got the better of me, and I looked at my phone.

It was an email, which wasn't Connor's style. If not Connor, who could it be? I ignored all the missed call notifications and went straight to the email. It was from the law firm, and it was a rather lengthy text, but my eyes zoomed in on one particular sentence.

We regret to inform you that your employment with us is hereby terminated.

My mouth fell open as I skimmed through the rest of the email.

Having tried and failed to get a hold of you several times over the past few days for a hearing with the firm, we have accepted that you are not interested in explaining yourself. After a thorough investigation into the events of the last function, we would have liked to give you a chance. However, your absence and silence are unacceptable, and we can no longer wait for you to return to the office.

I gulped the emotional lump that formed in my throat and scanned the missed call notifications. It turned out Connor hadn't been calling me, after all. They were all from the law firm.

My phone clattered to the floor shortly before I did, falling to my knees. If not for the soft, plush carpet, I might have hurt myself. As it was, I bent my head forward into my hands to stop the world from spinning around me. Bile threatened to rise in my throat, and I moved my arms to clutch my stomach instead.

How could I lose my job? I can't have lost my job.

With my thoughts all over the place, I didn't have the slightest inkling of what to do. There was only one constant; Connor. Somehow, I knew that Connor would know what to do. He would know how to help because, of course, he always did. He was always there when I needed him, always there to take care of me, and always a soothing balm to everything I dealt with. It had been that way long before we ever entered into our contract together. Despite everything, I knew that he cared about me. It wasn't lack of care that kept his name out of my notifications. On the contrary, it was the complete opposite. I'd asked him to give me space, and he'd respected my wishes.

And suddenly, I knew without complete and utter clarity that I needed him.

Once the thought entered my mind, I was like a woman possessed and no longer in control of the reins. I grabbed my keys, locked my place up, made a beeline for my car, and raced toward Connor's house. It was like someone else was moving my feet. Someone else lifted my hand. Someone else knocked on Connor's front door. Honestly, I could hardly remember how I got there at all. I was consumed by one thought, and one thought only.

I need my Daddy.

When the door finally opened, and I saw Connor's familiar strong features and his startling blue eyes, something inside me broke. It finally collapsed under the immense weight I'd been carrying for so long. The tears pricked and built up in my eyes, and I fell right into his arms.

I'd prepared to be rejected and to have the door slammed in my face. Connor would have been well within his rights to push me away, but he didn't. Instead, he held his arms open, and when I fell into them, he wrapped his arms around me tightly, holding me to his chest. The calm and steady sound of his heartbeat lulled me, and soon, my breathing and heart rate slowed to match up to his.

As if nothing ever happened between us, as if I'd seen him only the day before, he pulled me inside and closed the door behind us.

***

Connor took me inside, and we sat down in his living room.

"Are you ready to talk to me, baby girl?" His voice was gentle as if he were worried, I might break. I suppose I couldn't blame him. Tears were rolling down my cheeks.

"I got fired from the law firm this morning," I managed to mumble through sobs.

"It was all Lisa. She was the reason I couldn't talk to you. She told me that if I did that, she would know and make it worse for me," I explained.

"Lisa threatened to tell everyone about us, didn't she?" He was still gentle, but I could tell from the tightness of Connor's jaw that he was clenching his teeth.

"What did she have you do?" He asked. I sighed heavily.

"It was stupid, really. I basically had to act like her unpaid intern, get coffee for her, and act as if she were my boss. That sort of thing. It wouldn't have been so bad if not for the fact that I hated my job already and Lisa is a total bitch," I said. Connor flinched at the swear word, but I continued.

"You should have seen their faces, Daddy," I breathed out.

"Fuck them," Connor suddenly said. This time it was my turn to flinch, and I stared at him with wide eyes.

"I mean it. You don't need them. They're idiots and anyway, if you think about it, now you're finally free of them," he said.

"What do you mean?" I sniffed. Before he

responded, Connor stood and got a box of tissues from the other side of the room. He pulled one out and, instead of handing it to me, got down on his haunches in front of me and began wiping gently at my eyes and nose. While he cleaned me up, he continued.

"You hated that job, baby girl. It didn't suit you. The people were horrible, and the environment was stifling," he said. When he was done, he gave me a small smile. My eyes were still watery but no longer pouring.

"Think about it this way; you have the chance to spread your wings and do something you actually enjoy now," he continued.

"I guess," I mumbled. I wasn't quite sold on the idea, but he was right about one thing. Losing my job wasn't so bad, and I was kind of relieved that I'd never have to go back into the office again.

"You know, even through all this, I never stopped thinking about you. I'm sorry I hung up on you. I know now that I need you in my life," I said. Connor pressed the tip of his index finger against my lips.

"Shhh, it's okay. All is forgiven. Let Daddy take care of you," Connor said. Nodding my head, I submitted. At Connor's gentle guidance, I laid down on the couch, and he pressed a kiss to my forehead before disappeared into the kitchen. The sound of utensils and cutlery could be heard as he cooked, lulling me to sleep. After everything, I suddenly felt eerily calm, and I knew it was because of my Daddy.

When I woke from my nap, it was to the delicious smell of chicken soup. Connor had reappeared, and he took me into his arms, sitting me up as I came to. A bowl sat on the table, alongside a spoon. The moment I reached for them, however, Connor held me back.

"No, no," he murmured. I relaxed against his arms, gladly resting against his chest as he put a bib around my neck.

"I'm feeding you, little one," he said. Heat rushed to my cheeks as Connor grabbed the bowl whilst holding me in both arms. Slowly, he carried spoonful after spoonful into my mouth. The soup tasted even better than it smelled, and it warmed my body as it traveled down my throat. Once or twice, it spilled onto my chin and Connor would simply use the bib to wipe it off.

I wasn't sure I'd ever felt as at peace as I did at that moment. Little Space felt more like a home than anywhere else, especially when I was in my Daddy's arms, and although we'd practiced the kink for a while now, I wasn't sure I fully understood why Littles were so happy until this moment. It was as if I could melt into his arms and stay there forever.

Soon, however, the bowl was empty, and I was full. Connor set it down on the table, and we simply sat there for a while. He ran his fingers softly through my hair and rocked back and forth, threatening to make me fall asleep once again. For this moment, I was able to forget about everything.

That was until Connor slipped out from behind me and stood up. Before I could say or ask anything though, he slid his one arm behind the small of my back and the other arm beneath my knees. He picked me up as if I weighed nothing and carried me to the bathroom. I allowed myself to relax as Connor undressed me and ran me a nice hot bath. I thought it best not to mention that I already had a shower before I drove to his place. I wanted him to take care of me and the bubble bath, looked so good. Thus, I simply kept quiet and enjoyed the caregiving I was receiving.

Once the bath was full and Connor had checked the temperature of the water, he picked me up and lowered me into it. As sleepy as I was, I simply sank into the bubbles and sighed as their silkiness brushed across my skin. The next thing I knew, Connor grabbed a loofa and poured way too much body wash into it before washing my body. He treated me as if I were a fragile thing that might break at any minute, grazing the sponge along my back and down my legs with slow and methodical motions.

It can't get any better than this.

I was convinced that Connor was washing away

every single worry and care that plagued my existence, and I hummed with pleasure. This earned me another kiss on the forehead. For the first time in days, I smiled up at Connor.

"Is my little girl enjoying bath time?" He asked.

"Yes, Daddy. Thank you," I whispered.

"It's always a pleasure to take care of my baby girl," he said. Next, Connor washed my hair, and his fingers massaging my scalp felt so good that my eyes rolled back. All too soon, I was clean—thoroughly if one considered the shower I'd had beforehand—and Connor emptied the bathtub. He wrapped me up in a towel and once again lifted me up like I was nothing.

"You're like a mountain," I mumbled absent-mindedly, wrapping my arms around his shoulders. Connor grinned down at me.

"And what does that make you?" He asked.

"I don't know. I'm a leaf or something," I said.

"A leaf?" He asked, incredulously. Connor's

laugh was booming, echoing down the hallway and rumbling through his huge body.

"I think you're more like a butterfly or a cute little bird," he said. I pouted. My voice came out husky with sleep since I was already halfway into dreamland.

"A butterfly?" I asked.

"Mhmm," he hummed as we entered the bedroom.

"Because you're beautiful and full of color," he explained.

"Oh," I couldn't think of anything else to say, but I couldn't resist smiling at the thought of Connor thinking I was beautiful and full of color.

"See, beautiful," he nodded. The bed gave way beneath my tired body, and I got comfortable immediately as Connor set me down, but then he turned away and began to walk out of the room.

"Wait! Where are you going?" I called. I was rewarded with that look that he gave me, the one where his dimples appeared even though he wasn't smiling.

"I'll be right back, little one," he lovingly said.

"Oh," I settled back down. I needn't have worried because he wasn't away for too long and when he came back, it was with a blanket, a pacifier, and my favorite stuffie Peanut Butter. Surprised by how much joy I felt, I tried to conceal it even though I wanted to dance and giggle with giddiness. Connor took his place beside me and threw the blanket over us. His huge arms engulfed me next, and I was only too happy to settle against his chest. I looked up at him, my mouth open, and he slid the paci in. I bit down on it and sucked it gently as Connor passed me my stuffie. Content as could be, I let my heavy eyelids fall shut as I squeezed it tightly in my arms.

The slight rise and fall of Connor's chest as he took deep breaths in and out lulled me to sleep. Everything that had happened between us, at work, and in my room faded away. There was no thought, sound, or situation that could pull me from this contentedness. I thought that if it was like this for the rest of my life, then I wouldn't have minded in the slightest.

My Daddy knew exactly how to take care of me.

Chapter 9

The following morning brought trepidation and the familiar feelings I'd been wallowing in. Rather than feel the warm glow of happiness I'd basked in the previous evening, I was struck once more with the reminders of the awful past few days. I hated my memory instantly, wishing it were bad enough to let me be in peace at least for the first minutes of the day.

The curtains were open, and sunshine broke into the room in a thousand blinding rays. The first light of dawn caused me to pull the blanket over my head and shut my eyes tighter than ever. It didn't really do me any good. Sleep had already forsaken me, and I knew it was too late to slip back into the realm of dreams. Still, that didn't stop me from trying.

"Come on, baby girl," Connor's voice broke through the cover of my blanket, and I had to resist the urge to sigh.

What was the point? The world was much safer here in the safety of bed. I pulled the blankets around my shoulders tighter and turned over into the warmth of the bedsheets beneath me. As much as I didn't want to ignore Connor, there was something that just pulled me back into myself. My limbs felt slow and heavy, as if I was pressed into the mattress by some invisible force that insisted on keeping me there.

"Jessie," I heard Connor sigh before feeling the mattress dip under his weight behind me. He settled in next to me, and his hand landed on my shoulder gently, not saying anything for a few minutes as we laid there.

What was wrong? Was he not going to say or do anything? I was sure that he was going to punish me for not listening the first time, but he seemed rather resigned at this point.

It couldn't have been because of last night, could it? No, that wasn't it. Things were back to normal between the two of us when I came over, especially after apologizing for keeping everything involving Lisa from him. Besides, the man who cared for me and said all was forgiven didn't seem like a man who would switch back to being upset with me, if I thought about it. No, last night was filled with love.

I knew that one night was not enough to fix my entire life, but I had hoped that it would solve at least this part, this slice of heaven where I could feel safe and be myself again.

"Jessie," he tried again. I pulled the blanket down and turned my head up at him, taking in his warm hand, still resting over my shoulder.

"Are you okay, sweetheart?" He asked. If I had to be honest, I wasn't sure about how to express how I felt. One part of me was glad to be rid of that witch, realizing that Connor truly had been right about the people at my office being horrible, but another missed my job. It was familiar. There were always ups and downs that came with it, but I did like having some kind of routine. If nothing else, it was a reason to get out of bed. It was something that was mine. More than anything else, it certainly was a way of paying my bills. I had no idea how I was going to do that now.

"I'll be okay," was probably the most honest answer I could have given him. Finally, I rolled over to face that patient smile that made my insides melt. He leaned down and placed a reassuring kiss on my lips—nothing more than a feather-light brush—and rose to his feet, making my cheeks burn before the blankets around me were ripped away.

"Daddy!" I complained before rushing at them, trying to pull them back to the bed but Connor's grip held them far out of my reach, giant that he was.

He wasn't going to let it be that easily with that annoyingly sexy grin of his. If he wanted to play tug-of-war, he could bring it on. It wasn't a fair fight. Connor was bigger and stronger than I was. His hands practically covered half the material whereas mine only gripped at one small corner. That didn't stop me from trying though—at least until I lost my grip and went flying off the side of the bed with a cry of terror.

Connor didn't let me fall. The blanket was abandoned, dropped onto the floor, and I fell into his waiting arms. The force of momentum pushed us both to the floor, and I couldn't help but pout at having lost the battle. Connor, on the other hand, chuckled deeply as he held me close.

"You know, I could always climb back into bed without the blanket. It's totally still an option," I said. I let out a huff and got a light spank on my ass that made me flinch in response.

"Either you come out on your own, or I carry you down for breakfast. You know the rules," he chastised.

"Can I have it in bed today?" I asked.

"I think you've spent quite enough time in bed. At some point you'll have to remember what the rest of your apartment looks like, you know," he shook his head.

"Except this isn't *my* apartment," I pointed out.

"It'll be good practice for you," he answered

sternly, never missing a beat. My lips pressed together. As much as I was ready to argue that there was no forgetting my apartment, I knew he was right. I didn't want to admit how often I'd taken my food back to bed on the odd occasion that I did happen to get out of it.

"Yes, Daddy," I said. I walked behind him as we went to the kitchen where breakfast was already on the table. I had to admit it looked good. Plates filled with fluffy scrambled eggs and a couple of streaks of bacon sitting next to them waited for us. A separate plate with golden slices of toast looked too good to describe.

My stomach let out an appreciative grumble as we sat down, and the smell hit my nose. Connor let out a low chuckle. My cheeks warmed at the realization that my belly grumbled loud enough for him to hear it.

"Do you want me to heat it up again or would you rather not want to wait?" He asked. Before I could say anything, my stomach answered for me, making him laugh again.

"Well, that answers that. Go ahead and eat. I'll join you in a second," he laughed. There was something intimate about watching Connor moving around the kitchen as I ate at the table. It wasn't the first time, but there were times where I had been too wrapped up in Little mode to pay attention to these moments, moments when I realized just how attractive my *boyfriend* really was—my belly bubbled with giddiness that came out in a giggle that caused Connor to glance over his shoulder in silent question. I took in things like the way the hem of his shirt lifted when he reached for the coffee on the top shelf or how his hair seemed to reflect the light in just the right way, making the color more intense than I'd ever seen it before.

It was then that I realized it; I loved this man. The words flowed through me with every quickened heartbeat, getting stronger the longer my eyes stayed locked on him, even when he smiled upon catching me staring at him. That look took my breath away. I could have sworn that my inner self was ready to burst into flames once again, warmed by the sudden shock that I'd found the person I wanted to be with always as well as the fact that I was a completely different person from the one who walked into the bar to complain about work only a short while ago.

"Jessie don't play with your food," Connor's voice echoed in my little bubble as he sat down with his own plate in front of him, bringing me back from my daydream.

"Sorry, Daddy," I murmured, shifting. I looked down at my hands to see that I'd been pushing around the last bit of my eggs. Did I really eat everything and not realize it? I guess I really *was* hungry. I settled back to my eggs, grabbing a slice of toast to scoop the remainder onto as Connor sipped his coffee. We ate in silence for a few moments before Connor cleared his throat.

"The past few days haven't been easy for you. And as much as you'll probably want to argue with me, I'm concerned about you, especially with regards to what you're going to do with your life now," he started. The thoughts had crossed my mind. Of course, they had. I was especially concerned about the apartment. It was almost the end of the month and even if they were willing to give me the last month's rent, how was I going to afford the next month? What about the student loans that I still had to pay off or even food? Things weren't exactly cheap these days, and even though I had some money in my savings account, that wasn't going to last for very long. My boss may have been a hotshot lawyer, but that didn't mean he paid much.

The idea of finding another job, however, made my stomach twist. I was never good at that part. I recalled an embarrassing moment when I'd applied to a fast food restaurant to earn some extra cash while I was studying—the manager thought I was asking him on a date and I walked away with his number on the back of a napkin, alongside a sly wink as he passed me a handful of free packets of sauce.

"Jessie, listen to me for a sec before those

wheels go taking you far away again. I didn't mean to send you on a thought tangent, but there was something I wanted to say. As much as you were attached to your job at that company, I don't think that going back would be the best idea. Especially with that woman still there," Connor continued as those eyes of his observed her over his coffee mug. It was true. Even if I did go back, there was no guarantee that Lisa wasn't going to start trouble again. Not to mention that there were other people in the company who knew my secret and chances were that many of them wouldn't let me forget about it that easily. If I had learned anything in my lifetime, it was that humans were unnecessarily cruel to each other. That and people who were different or unusual got it even worse than the rest.

"What am I supposed to do then, Daddy?" I asked quietly. Connor's gaze softened at my question. It must have come out a little more childlike than either of us expected from me lately, but that was what he was there for. He was my guide, among other things, and no one could put me at ease like he could.

"Well, picking yourself up and trying again is step one. I'll help you look for a new job if you want me to, but you're a big girl and being able to start over after something like this shows me that. Things will be better when you find a place where you actually fit in. Even though you're still my little girl and I'll be there for you as much as you need, you still have responsibilities outside of us." he said, putting down his mug and took one of my hands in between his bigger ones as he looked into my eyes.

I nodded before I felt warm, wet tears trickling down my face as my free hand closed around the fabric of my pajamas as if the motion itself was going to hold myself together. Why? Why were those words enough to make me cry? Before all of this, the idea of starting over seemed a pleasant one, but there was something about this situation that struck somewhere in the middle of my chest. I didn't quite know where the tears were coming from, only that they wouldn't stop.

Connor hooked his other arm around my waist and pulled me to him, positioning me on his lap with my head nestled in the crook of his shoulder before I had the chance to realize what was happening. It must be fun being a giant; they get huge things done in tiny amounts of time. His hand rubbed my back gently as I breathed in his familiar scent, both setting me at ease.

"Remember, you don't have to hold yourself back in front of me," he murmured. So, I did. The stress of everything that had been happening welled up inside of me, coming out once again as I relished in the comfort and safety of Connor's embrace. I could stay in his arms always. No matter how many times the thought occurred to me, I didn't think I would ever stop being amazed at how much better having a Daddy like Connor made me feel about myself and my life.

Although I have to admit, I didn't remember when I'd become such a cry baby. By the time I stopped sobbing long enough to wipe my tears, I was sure that Connor's legs had fallen asleep with the dining chair beneath the two of us. He didn't let on that he was the slightest bit uncomfortable, which only made me happier.

"Are you feeling better, sweetheart?" He finally asked me. And I was sure that for the first time in days, I was.

***

"I had an idea that I wanted to bring up with you during breakfast," Connor told me while helping me make the bed. Connor was supposed to head to work soon, but he decided to call in to say that he was running late due to an emergency. It was sweet to think that he would do that to make sure that I was okay even though I told him that he didn't need to.

"I suppose now is as good a time as any. What would you say about us living together?" he asked. All at once, I'd transformed into a bundle of nerves, set off by his words, barely managing to contain myself. I tucked in the sheet and set up the pillows, placing Peanut Butter right in front. He looked like such a happy little bear, and I smiled as I turned to Connor and tried my best to keep my voice even.

"What do you mean? Like, me moving in with you?" I questioned wanting clarification.

He nodded.

"It would be temporary, but yes. At least so you can save some money until you find another job. I mean, you spend a lot of time here anyway. This way, you wouldn't have to worry about some things," he explained.

"Okay," I said in a small voice, I didn't have to think about it for very long, this was an easy decision.

***

With Connor's help, it took another week or so for me to pack up my apartment. My furniture and some of the larger things were moved into storage while my clothes and the smaller things like the stuffed animals that he'd given me accompanied me to his apartment. There were so many grown-up actions that needed to be done, responsibilities that simply had to be seen to. Thankfully, my landlords were understanding about my moving out on short notice. They had given me extra time to pay off the lease cancellation fees and the last month's rent. Hopefully, I would find a way to make some money before then.

I was on my own for the drive there, and my stomach had a knot sitting in the middle of it. It was a really big change compared to going to Connor's—no, *our*—apartment before this. There used to be just a simple overnight bag that I kept in case I went over to his for a play session, but now.

Now there was no need for that. We'd be living together.

The thought both made me excited and nervous. I knew that I'd be seeing other sides of Connor now, sides I'd never seen before. There were things that one only found out about another person upon living with them. How did he keep the bathroom? Did he actually do dishes even when he wasn't expecting company? Were the cushions on the sofa always fluffed? This was going to be a learning experience and a half, for both of us.

When I got to the apartment, I was grateful that Connor had already had the good sense to remember to give me a key to let myself in while he was out—something I'd never have remembered on my own. It was much neater than I remember it being the last time I was there, not that it wasn't neat the last time, but I could swear even the scent had changed. There was that familiar scent of lemons that came with most generic cleaning supplies.

A jangle of keys sounded from the other side of the front door, and it opened to reveal Connor holding a covered box in his hands. My brows knitted together as he carried it over to the table and set it down, smiling at me in that way he did when he gave me presents.

"Hey, baby girl, all settled in?" He asked as he came over and gave me an affectionate kiss on the forehead. Before he could move away, my hands caught his waist and pulled him back for a proper one, tilting my head all the way back to meet his towering form. He pulled away with a sexy chuckle and gestured toward the box. Tugging my lower lip between my teeth, I ventured over to the table, raising the cover off the box and staring up at me with dark chocolate eyes cuter than buttons was a small white bunny rabbit. Its clean, white fur looked softer than anything I had ever touched before. It was so tiny with a twitching nose, and its beady eyes never moved from me, looking up with curiosity. When I reached out to give it a pet, I was excited to find out that I was right. My heart was warm, and I was beaming with pure happiness. It was like touching a cloud.

"I can see you love her already," Connor rubbed my back gently as I pet the bunny. I looked at the little fluff ball, and my heart melted as, under my gentle pets, it decided to curl up to go to sleep on the small blanket that was in the corner of the box.

"Thank you so much for the gift, Daddy!" I

squealed. He just laughed, looking rather pleased with himself for the choice of gift.

"Would you like to go shopping for supplies for her later? She'll need a proper hutch we can put in the garden and food if we're going to keep her," Connor explained. I nodded enthusiastically, simply eager to both spend any time with him, as well as provide some comfort for our new family member.

"Have you thought of a name for her yet?" Connor asked.

"I'll call her Cloud," I giggled as I kissed her head.

Chapter 10

"Are you ready for this?" Connor asked. We were sitting on the plush carpet—my choice—in his living room. I was happily curled up in his arms, doodling in a notebook, while he worked on our brand-new contract. It seemed he was finally done because the sound of his fingers flying across the keyboard had ceased, and he was pressing soft kisses to the curve between my neck and shoulder, making me giggle like a little girl.

"Daddy! That tickles!" I exclaimed.

"C'mon, Jessie, I can't read it without you," Connor said.

"Okay, okay," I said, I knew what my name meant in this particular case. I put my notebook down and sat up straighter. Since I lost my job, it was rare to find me out of Little Space. He turned the screen for me to look at the document he'd spent days typing up for us, taking in every tiny consideration.

"Is it all done? This is our new contract?" I asked.

"It is indeed," Connor replied. I began reading through our new terms. Connor told me that we had to reevaluate since I was living with him now. Based on the fact that our dynamic had changed, it made sense. All of the previous rules and agreements were still there. Neither of us had issues with the things we'd tried so far. There were simply a number of additions to be made.

Be waiting for Daddy after his shift. That one made me light up.

"It's totally the best way to wind down after work," I grinned at Connor.

"I can't argue with you there," he said.

Take care of Cloud during the day. This one needn't have been added. I adored my rabbit and feeding, bathing, and playing with her gave me great joy. I even enjoyed cleaning her cage because she would twitch her little nose and hop over to me to check out what I was doing every time. Still, it made me feel better to know I had daily responsibilities.

Do your chores. Connor helped me make the bed in the mornings, but I still had to do laundry and clean up after myself.

No dessert before dinner. I flushed. It was only one time, one occasion where Connor had gotten home earlier than expected to find me eating ice cream before dinner. I'd been punished for the simple fact that I looked guilty enough to know I shouldn't have been doing it.

Bathe in the evening with Daddy. I pressed my thighs together at the thought. It turned out Connor quite liked it when I washed his back. I'd done it once, and now it was a rule.

Some of the other rules were ones that were pretty obvious but needed to be written down, just in case I decided to be bratty according to Connor. His logic was that I might be deterred if I knew punishment was a consequence. Most of the time, this was true. My nature couldn't be helped, though. There were times where I found myself giving Connor attitude without even meaning to.

Don't backtalk.

Don't swear.

Don't lie.

Don't steal.

Don't break things.

Do art at least once a day. That was one we hadn't discussed before.

"Once a day?" I asked.

"Mhmm. You're an incredibly talented artist, Jessie. I don't want you squandering it. Plus, I love it when you paint and draw things for me," Connor said.

"You really love it?" I asked. Connor pulled me in and pressed a kiss to the top of my head.

"Of course, I do, sweetheart. I'm not just saying that. You have some serious skills, especially considering you've never taken classes," he said. Smiling, I returned my attention to the list. Apart from all the items on the previous contract, I couldn't see much else to approve. I navigated to the clipart in the document and placed one giant tick over the entire thing, eliciting a chuckle from Connor that vibrated through my body as he wrapped his arms around me and pulled me near.

***

The following day was the first under our new contract, and I had a to-do list pinned to the fridge. As soon as I woke up, I went to check it out. If there was one thing that made getting out of bed in the morning easier, it was that I didn't need to go to work. The pile of pancakes waiting for me in the oven weren't bad either. Connor made breakfast before leaving.

I munched on one chocolate chip pancake while reading through the list on the fridge. Connor hadn't helped me write it, but I'd shown it to him after I wrote it. He approved wholeheartedly, and that's when he stuck it on the fridge for me. Perhaps I would be more productive if I composed such lists on a daily basis. As it was, I had quite a few things to do.

Eating was first, and showering was next. After that, I had to clean the hutch and feed Cloud. I hurried through my breakfast and raced toward the bathroom. Yet another benefit of living with

Connor was that his shower was big enough that I could sing to my heart's content. I only ever sang and danced when he was at work though. I wasn't quite confident enough to let him hear me.

It occurred to me after I'd showered and put on some adult clothes, a pair of jeans and a black tank top, that life truly had improved since Lisa's vindictive act. I never expected it, but I was living the life of my dreams. The only thing that kind of sucked was the job hunt. That was the biggest thing on my to-do list, as it had been every single other day. I didn't know how there were so many jobs posted on a daily basis, and yet, no one had called me back. A part of me began to wonder if people were calling my previous employers. It would explain an awful lot.

I didn't like that thought, so I shrugged it off and headed to the garden, where Cloud was happily sleeping in her hutch.

"Hey girl," I murmured as I pulled her out. She curled up closer in my arms, not yet ready to be woken up.

I set her down in the grass so she could run around for a bit, something I was only allowed to do if I supervised her and got down to cleaning the hutch. The only problem was that Cloud did not want to run about. One would think a rabbit would be happy for the chance to bounce around, but no. She was quite content to watch me. She was the stillest rabbit I'd ever seen, and it was hard not to notice how different we were. I struggled to stay still for too long. That might have been why Connor gave me so much to do at home, especially since I didn't have a job.

"You're a strange girl," I shook my head, replacing her bed with a clean one. Next, I picked Cloud up and took her inside so that I could fill up her water and food bowls. Only there did she start hopping about, making her way over to Connor's sofa and sniffing at it before moving toward the CD rack. The first time I'd seen his collection of CDs, I asked Connor how old he was. He laughed, but I knew I'd offended him when he started explaining that most of them belonged to his mother. That explained the Neil Diamond.

When I was done putting the food and water back outside, Cloud decided she didn't want to go back in her cage. She hopped out of my way every time I went toward her, and for a rabbit that didn't spend much time inside, she seemed to know exactly how to get away from me. I chased her for several minutes until a stitch formed in my side, reminding me just how unfit I was.

"That's it," I gasped, making my way back into the kitchen. I knew I had Cloud the moment I entered the living room because her nose began twitching like crazy. I waved the carrot around in the air, dangling it quite literally.

"Do you want it?" I said.

Cloud's nose twitched, and she took one hesitant hop toward me and then another. Getting down on my haunches, I simply took tiny steps toward her until we met halfway. As cute and fluffy as she was, Cloud did not mess around when it came to carrots. She chomped it out of my hand forcefully and began devouring it.

With a grin on my face, I took the chance to pick her up, careful to catch the end of the carrot so that she didn't drop it.

"I think that's enough excitement for one day," I murmured as I put her back in the hutch. I sat with her for a while, gently stroking her soft fur and mentally thanking Connor. If not for Cloud, I knew I'd be a rather lonely Little while he was at work.

Chapter 11

The days passed by and with them, the seasons began to change. Fall had come, bringing with it overcast mornings that made me want to stay in bed and watch movies all day. The shades of amber could be found everywhere, including in the brand-new necklace Connor bought me.

"It suits you," he commented.

"I always thought you'd be more of a spring girl," he said. I raised my eyebrows.

"With the way, I don't want to get out of bed?" I questioned.

"Fair enough, you've got me there. Can I see what you're painting?" He asked. We were in the room where all my Little things were kept. It became a den of sorts, similar to Connor's study. This was where I painted and wrote during the day. I inclined my head, and Connor came around to stand on the other side of the easel. The painting was a depiction of the garden outside, with orange and red leaves blowing in the wind along the grass. The old oak was devoid of leaves, leaning creepily with its branches curling like fingers. Cloud could be seen near the roots that broke through the ground, happily nibbling on a carrot. I could almost hear the rustle of the leaves as I looked at the painting. It was one of my favorites to date.

"Oh, wow," Connor murmured. I'd been painting every day as per my rules, and I could definitely see an improvement There was something genuine about Connor complimenting my art that made everything seem more real. I could always tell he was being honest.

"You really think so?" I asked, just in case.

"Jessie, I think you need to start sending your art to places. Let me help you create a portfolio and start sending it out," he said.

"You mean like, to galleries and stuff?" I was doubtful.

"I do. You've been looking for work for a while, right? You've technically been doing work every single day," he said.

I bit down on my lower lip, looking back at the painting. Maybe it wouldn't be such a bad idea after all.

"Okay. Will you help me?" I finally said. Connor's smile warmed my heart.

"Of course, I will," he said. We were silent for some time as I packed away my art supplies. Connor's return from work usually meant the end of my creative pursuits and settling into the sofa to watch something together. We didn't really do much else these days.

"Jessie, I wanted to talk to you about something," Connor started once I was finished.

"Did I do something wrong?" I said as I turned to him, instantly guilty.

"Why would you think that?" Connor asked as he shook his head and waved it off.

"Wait, don't worry. You aren't in trouble," he said.

"Then what's going on?" I asked. He walked over to me, running a nervous hand through his hair.

"I've noticed that you've been a bit different these past few weeks. Apart from painting, you don't really do much else. I mean, there's nothing wrong with that, but..." He sighed, struggling to find the words. I heaved a sigh. This wasn't a conversation I thought would ever actually come up, and now that it was here, I wasn't sure how to tell Connor what was really going on with me. I went over to my painting seat, as equally at a loss for words as Connor had been a few moments earlier. The truth was nothing was wrong. We lived a perfectly good life. I might even get to have my art in a gallery if this portfolio thing went well.

"Please don't shut me out again," Connor said when I hadn't answered for a while.

"I'm bored," I blurted out.

"Bored? Bored with me?" His brows knitted together. Standing, I went over to him and took his hands.

"Of course I'm not bored with you, Daddy," I said. The look of sadness and confusion on his face broke my heart a tiny bit.

"I'm bored with life right now. When we first got together, everything was new and exciting. I miss that feeling. Take today for instance. I knew we were gonna go out there and watch something while snuggling on the sofa and while that's nice and all, I really miss the thrill of not knowing what was coming next. You know?" I tried to explain. Connor stared at me, and his silence only prompted me to talk more.

"I mean, we haven't been to another play party in a while. And sure, we changed the contract up, but that was months ago. Every day is predictable," I said. The tension in the room sparked, and my heart got a bit faster with each second that ticked by in silence. I hoped I hadn't said anything wrong. I wanted to simply ask Connor to say something, but of course I couldn't do that. So, I sat in my seat, watching him and sweating from nervousness.

"Well, how are you feeling about us?" He finally asked.

"Oh, Daddy, there's nothing wrong with us. I still love you. I just want a little more excitement, you know?" I said. Instead of answering me, Connor walked over and cupped my face with his hands. He leaned in and pressed his lips to mine. The suddenness, the pure passion of his kiss, made butterflies swirl in my stomach. I reached for his waist and pulled him closer, giving into the kiss with a small sigh in the back of my throat.

When he pulled away, I was breathless, and my lips felt swollen.

"I love you too," he whispered. Before I could freak out, Connor leaned in and dragged his lips along my neck, making me forget how words worked.

"I love you, little one," he said again.

"Daddy," I murmured. I couldn't believe I told him I loved him. I smiled demurely, feeling as if I could have floated upward and off of my chair in that moment. My heart was happy. I was happy.

"So, what do you think you're looking for, little miss?" He asked.

"It's been a while since you called me that," I commented. He gave me a moment to think it over.

"I guess, you know, some stuff to spice up our relationship. I... Uhm, I read about, like, impact play," I said smirking.

"Impact play?" Connor said, raising an eyebrow.

"Yeah, and uhm... Also like, training. Stuff like deepthroating," I stammered. It was so much easier to think and read about it than to talk about it. With every word I said, my neck got hotter and hotter. I was glad my hair was loose for the simple fact that it covered my ears because I was pretty sure they were as red as tomatoes.

"You want me to train you?" Connor finally asked. I bit down on my lower lip, nodding.

"You know, I happen to have a paddle in my bedroom if you really want to play with impact," he said.

"A paddle?" I breathed. Connor nodded his head, staring down at my lip.

"Wait here. And take your clothes off. I'll be right back," he said. My heart was racing as he ran off. I paused only for a moment before taking my top off. The next thing to go were my jeans. I couldn't waste a second. I may have wanted to try impact play, but I wasn't sure how much pain I could handle. It was better not to disobey my Daddy.

When he came back into the room, Connor held a bright purple paddle in his hand.

"Good girl. Bend over the chair," Connor said.

"Yes, Daddy," I said gulping as I did as I was told. I took a deep breath, telling myself that this was all about trust. If I didn't trust him, there was no way this relationship would work. Connor didn't smack me suddenly. I felt the paddle brush against the curve of my ass, cold enough that I flinched away from it. Connor paused until I settled back again. Without warning, the paddle came down on my ass, warm and hard. It barely felt like anything. Connor repeated on the other side before coming back. He was true to his word. Each spank was soft and gentle, but the longer he went on, the more it stung.

I almost didn't notice that they were getting harder and harder, but I knew without seeing it that my ass was bright red. To my utter surprise, my pussy was so wet it was dripping down the inside of my thighs. Each time Connor brought the paddle down, I could feel the sensation hitting me right in my center, in my most sensitive of parts.

"Are you okay?" Connor paused, right when I thought I wouldn't be able to handle anymore, and my safe word was hanging off the tip of my tongue. I nodded.

"Sweetheart, I'm going to need you to use your big girl words," he said.

"Yes, Daddy!" I cried out, clenching my ass cheeks. Once Connor stopped, all feeling returned to me.

"Do you want to stop?" Connor asked. I nodded my head, which awarded me with Connor's gentle hands as he stroked my ass comfortingly.

"Do you want to do something else?" He asked.

"I want to suck your cock," I whispered. I didn't usually speak dirty. That was Connor's job.

"Ask for Daddy's permission," he said. Something about the fact that I couldn't actually see him made me even hotter: my pussy pulsed and I moaned. I took a deep breath before I spoke.

"Daddy?" I asked.

"Yes, baby girl?" He sounded as breathless as I did.

"Please, can I swear?" I asked.

"Just this once," Connor whispered as if he were afraid of breaking the intensity of the moment. My pussy clenched again.

"Please, can you fuck my throat?" I asked.

"Oh, God, little one," Connor moaned. He moved around in front of me and unbuckled his belt and jeans, freeing his hard-on. It bounced out so excitedly that I giggled and that only drove Connor crazier. I could see it written all over his face as he reached forward to stroke my hair.

I looked up to find that he was checking out my ass, still on display in this bent-over position, while holding his cock in one hand. He moved forward until the head touched my lips and I opened my mouth eagerly, allowing him to slide in until he reached the back of my throat in one smooth movement.

It was impossible not to gag, and the second I did, Connor pulled back slightly. I swirled my tongue all around his shaft, paying special attention to the underside. All the while, I kept my eyes glued to his facial expressions. My favorite part about sucking Connor off was the pleasure that it gave him. Don't get me wrong, other things did that too, but there was some kind of power that came with having him in my mouth. It was the one part of the relationship where I felt truly in charge, the one part where I didn't choose to give him all the control.

"Oh, you like that, do you?" Connor whispered.

"You like Daddy fucking your throat? You're such a good little girl," he added. My pussy responded to his words, and I sucked even harder. Drool dripped down my chin, but I didn't care. I wanted him to know what his words were doing to me, what he was doing to me.

"I want you to relax, baby girl. When I move forward, just relax and breathe through your nose like you normally do," he said. I tried. As hard as it was, my body felt overloaded with sensation, I relaxed. I breathed through my nose. Connor took slow, shallow thrusts while I did, letting me get used to it.

"That's it," he commented in his proud-of-you voice, stroking my hair with one hand. The other reached forward and slapped my ass cheek. He muffled my cry as he reached over and repeated the action. His arms were so damn long that he could reach my pussy while in my mouth. I couldn't help lifting my ass up so he could get a better angle, which in turn made him slide into my throat.

Connor was fully in my throat; every last inch of him buried in my mouth. My eyes widened as his balls touched my chin, and he released a grunt of pure ecstasy. At the same moment, I felt two fingers slide into me easily. This was the wettest I'd ever been, and I could barely contain myself. Somehow, his fingers pumping in and out of me made me want to suck his dick even harder and so I did, eliciting yet another groan.

"Oh, fuck," he murmured. And the next thing I knew, Connor was pumping in and out of my mouth like a piston. I could do nothing but take it as he used my mouth. Sometimes I gagged, and when I did, he pulled out for only a moment to let me catch my breath before reentering. More often than not, he made it easily into my throat. I couldn't keep my eyes on him anymore; they were shut as he fingered me as fast and hard as he was fucking my mouth. With every stroke, I could feel my orgasm building and the fact that I was letting Connor use me while I reached the peak only made it hotter.

Connor reached forward with his other hand, releasing my head so that he could stroke and squeeze my ass while he fucked my throat. The moans I made around him, sending vibrations through the length of his cock, drove him crazy. I could tell because that's when his thrusts grew more erratic. My whole body was alight with pleasure, and I wanted to scream when I finally felt my body give in. Tiny sparks of electricity flooded toward my pussy and my cry of pure pleasure was drowned out by the cock in my mouth.

The second I came, Connor moved his hands to hold the back of my head. He stared down at my face as he pumped in and out and I knew it was because having me in this position, so vulnerable and willing, was exactly what was getting him off in that moment. I fluttered my eyelashes and sucked my cheeks in as hard as I could, the hollows obvious as I flicked my tongue along his shaft.

Finally, he began whispering my name and threw

his head back, shutting his eyes as he forced his way forward one last time. I felt his cock twitch in my mouth, and then one, two, three spurts of his cum went straight down my throat. I had no choice but to swallow as quickly as I could, eagerly trying to gulp down every last drop as he sighed and moaned above me. Some of it escaped, joining my spit in dripping out of the corners of my mouth and down my chin.

When he slid out of my throat, he immediately got down on his haunches, so his face was level with mine. He cupped it and began showering my face with kisses before pulling back to look at me. He was beaming with pride.

"Are you okay?" He asked.

"Never better," I smiled back. I shifted and realized the chair had been digging into me slightly. Connor answered by kissing me on the lips, and I gave into his tenderness, closing my eyes and enjoying the moment until he broke away.

"You are such a good girl," he said as I

giggled with pride.

"How about we get you bathed, huh? And I'll put you into a clean diaper, and we can cuddle," Connor said.

"Yes, please," I whispered. Connor led me into the bathroom and ran me a bubble bath, helping me climb into the warm water. He reached for a washcloth and gently washed away our session, the cum, and the pain. There was nothing sexual about this bath. Daddy was simply taking care of me, gentle as ever as he moved the washcloth over every inch of me. When he was done, he washed and conditioned my hair, making it into shapes that had me in fits of giggles that splashed him with water. His eyes were filled with love when he looked down at me, and I knew that he meant what he had said earlier.

After I was squeaky clean, Connor fetched one of the soft towels and held it out for me. He wrapped me up like a caterpillar and dried me off while I squirmed.

"Daddy!" I exclaimed.

"Do you want me to moisturize you, baby girl?" He asked. I nodded my head vigorously. Especially after spanks, this was one of my favorite ways to be cared for. Connor unwrapped me and got the moisturizer, lathering his hands up and rubbing down every part of me. He paid special attention to my butt cheeks, which I could feel were red from the spanks.

"Wow, sweetheart. Are you okay?" He muttered.

"I'm fine, Daddy. I liked the impact play," I replied.

"I wanna get dressed by myself tonight," I said when he was done putting a heart sticker right on the front of the diaper.

"Oh, you do? When did you become such a big girl?" He asked. I smiled, earning myself a raspberry on my belly. Connor ruffled my hair and went out to the kitchen. After that, I pulled on the first onesie I ever got and grabbed Peanut Butter before heading out into the kitchen.

A cup of hot chocolate was already waiting for me,

steamy and creamy with marshmallows floating on top. I held my arms out and Connor, who had gotten dressed in my absence, lifted me up onto the counter, holding me in an embrace for a moment longer than he really needed to. Afterward, he passed me my hot chocolate.

"Careful. Use both hands," he instructed. I watched Connor bustle around the kitchen, preparing pancakes for us, and my toes curled with wonder. He smiled and walked over to me, brushing strands of damp hair out of my face.

"You know, our anniversary is coming up. I was thinking of taking you on holiday, maybe somewhere with the Eiffel Tower. What do you say?" He asked.

"Daddy! I love Paris!" I exclaimed.

"You do?" Connor leaned in to kiss the top of my head.

"Well then, Paris it is. But first, I want to get your portfolio out there into the world. My little girl is too talented to be cooped up in here," he said.

"You really think my art is that good?" I asked sipping my drink.

"Sweetheart, I want to tell you something, but you have to promise not to be mad," he said hesitantly. Connor ran a hand through his hair.

"I may have already sent one or two photos of your art out to a gallery in France," he confessed.

"What did they say?!" I set my hot chocolate down, staring at him.

"They loved it. They want to see your portfolio," he whispered. I was so excited I wanted to bounce up and down. I settled for a little dance on the counter, which made Connor smile affectionately.

"Oh, my gosh. Please tell me you're not joking," I said.

"That's why I want to take you to France for our anniversary," he said. Tears welled up in my eyes as I stared up at him.

"Daddy, you are perfect," I said, looking up at him.

"No baby girl, you are perfect," Connor said, kissing me on my cheek.

Who is Tina Moore?

Tina Moore has enjoyed the lifestyle of a Mommy Domme for several years. She began exploring kink and BDSM in her youth and found her love of being a strict Mommy Domme in early 2000. Tina Moore is now an author of many MDLG, DDLG and ABDL themed novels.

Follow her on:

Author Page on Amazon

Instagram @tinamoore.kdp

If you enjoyed this book, it would be much appreciated if you leave **a review on Amazon**.

www.ingramcontent.com/pod-product-compliance
Lightning Source LLC
Chambersburg PA
CBHW030705190726
48286CB00001B/175